THE ICON OF THE CZAR

Alex loves her job as a tour leader, taking groups of holidaymakers to St Petersburg, in Russia. But she is not at all pleased when she finds that Richard, her ex-boyfriend, has been assigned to her group as assistant. Richard, though, proves he can be of great help when one of the group begins behaving mysteriously and risks putting Alex's future in jeopardy.

Books by Betty O'Rourke
in the Linford Mystery Library:

ISLAND OF THE GODS

BETTY O'ROURKE

THE ICON
OF THE CZAR

Complete and Unabridged

LINFORD
Leicester

First Linford Edition
published 1998

British Library CIP Data

O'Rourke, Betty
The icon of the Czar.—Large print ed.—
Linford mystery library
1. Detective and mystery stories
2. Large type books
I. Title
823.9′14 [F]

ISBN 0–7089–5351–4

Published by
F. A. Thorpe (Publishing) Ltd.
Anstey, Leicestershire
Set by Words & Graphics Ltd.
Anstey, Leicestershire
Printed and bound in Great Britain by
T. J. International Ltd., Padstow, Cornwall

This book is printed on acid-free paper

1

'The 747 from Heathrow has landed. Your people will be here in about ten minutes.' The airport official spoke to her in slow, careful English. He knew Alex understood Russian but he enjoyed the rare opportunity of practising his language skills. It was also pleasant to have an excuse to speak to the pretty English girl, with her long, blonde hair and creamy, rose-petal complexion.

Alex smiled and thanked him, then, shivering, pulled her jacket more closely round her slim frame. The arrivals hall at St Petersburg airport was, on this May evening, a bleak, draughty place, quite unlike any of the international airports of western Europe. The peeling walls and high, dingy ceilings with their crumbling plaster mouldings, made the place look like a derelict stately home. She hoped it wouldn't give a bad first impression to the group she had come to meet. This was the point at which she invariably felt a wave of panic engulf her. Here was a group of people, strangers to herself and each other, for whom she was entirely responsible for the next seven days. In that time, anything might happen; someone might fall ill, be involved in a street accident, or wander off and become hopelessly lost What if something like that happened this week? Would she really be able to cope?

To distract herself, she chatted to the two women customs officers manning the luggage X-ray machine. Alex, too, enjoyed any opportunity to speak Russian. She was fluent by now, though not helped by the fact that most of her time here she spoke English with the tourists who came for a week's cultural experience of Russia's second city.

Alex had studied Russian at school, as an alternative to the more popular languages on offer, and became fascinated by the literature, history and customs of the country. When she left, she'd wanted to make use of her language skill, but the obvious job, as interpreter in some government capacity, hadn't appealed. Then she heard about Offbeat Tours Ltd., a travel company offering holidays in the more unusual places of the world. They were a new company planning to offer, amongst other tours, short trips to Russia. Alex, with her language skills and enthusiasm for the country, was their ideal as a tour leader. Now she was waiting for her first group of British travellers for the year, for the spring tour of St. Petersburg.

She heard the baggage handlers trundling their trolleys into a side alcove beyond the customs desks and heard voices as the first passengers entered the far side of the building, but they sounded as if they were Russian.

Alex pulled her clipboard from her handbag. She'd be expected to know everyone's name by the end of the evening; better begin now and try to identify them as they came through the last customs check, the luggage X-ray machines.

There weren't many on this week's tour; fifteen altogether, mainly husband

and wife couples according to her company's briefing notes, though there were two retired lady schoolteachers travelling together and a mother with a daughter in her thirties. There was also one lady travelling alone, but no details had been given, beyond her name, a Miss Jane Chandler. Alex made a mental note to look out for the lone traveller and make sure she wasn't left out of any social activities. Probably she'd turn out to be an inveterate globe trotter, though she could just as easily be a quiet, self-effacing elderly lady who would be overlooked and ignored by the others unless she was looked after. It was part of the tour leader's job to ensure that single travellers didn't return home feeling their holiday had been a lonely and unsatisfying experience.

Alex turned over her clipboard and held it above her head. On it, the words 'Offbeat Tours' in large letters, acted as a rallying point for her new clients. A few Russian businessmen wearing astrakan hats came through the barrier and walked off with their hand luggage.

Unexpectedly, an English voice hailed her from behind them: 'Alex! Fifteen passengers for you coming through right now, safely delivered.'

'Richard!' Alex stared in amazement, tinged with dismay, at the young man coming through the barrier towards her. He was tall and fair-haired, a pleasant, open-faced young man of about her own age. His broad smile showed that he, at least, was pleased to see her there.

'What on earth are you doing here?' Alex demanded. 'I wasn't expecting they'd send you out with my group.'

'Sorry if I've disappointed you, then,' he replied, hoisting his suitcase from the conveyor belt beyond the X-ray machine and moving aside for the other passengers behind him. He came up to Alex and continued 'I'm afraid you're stuck with me breathing down your neck for the week. The company's sent me over as a second tour leader.'

'Two of us? But we don't need two for this tour. They'll be in the coach being driven around for most of the time,' Alex protested.

'I'm sure you don't need me, but the Director thought I should come out with this group so I can study what you do and learn as much as I can. It seems he's planning to expand the Russian tours and needs another tour leader who's familiar with the country and people.'

'I can hardly argue with the Director, I suppose,' Alex said with a shrug. 'How's your Russian?'

He made a face. 'Passable, but not anything like as good as yours. I'll leave you to deal with the natives.'

Alex tut-tutted. 'You'll never become fluent if you don't practise.' She assumed an innocent expression and added 'They do say the best way to learn a foreign language is to acquire a local girl-friend — '

'No, thanks!' Richard replied swiftly. 'Women have caused me enough trouble already. I'm steering clear of everything except purely business contacts with women from now on.'

Alex raised her eyebrows. 'Indeed?' she asked pointedly. 'That's not like you. I'd have thought — '

'Anyway, we'll be too busy for any personal social life, won't we? Starting now. They're all through customs so perhaps we should go over and introduce ourselves. Or, at least, you should. I spoke to most of them on the plane.'

Alex walked over to the small group standing uncertainly by the entrance doors. 'Welcome to St Petersburg, on behalf of Offbeat Tours,' she announced, with a smile that attempted to include all of them. 'I'm Alex Vincent, your tour leader for the week. Richard Evans here, I gather some of you have already met on the plane. We hope you'll have an enjoyable week in my favourite city. We plan to show you as much of it as we can possibly pack into the time and I guarantee you'll have some wonderful memories to take home with you. If you have any questions or problems, please ask Richard or myself and we'll do our best to sort things out. Now, if you'd like to follow me, our bus is waiting outside to take us to the Pribaltiyskaya hotel.'

Dutifully, the group trailed after her and Richard towards the parking area outside, virtually deserted now except for their tour bus, parked prominently in the centre.

As they filed on board, Alex whispered to Richard 'Which one is Miss Chandler?'

'Dunno. Never found out their names,' Richard shrugged.

Alex sighed. Well, it would probably become clear once they'd settled themselves in the seats. She climbed aboard last and picked up the microphone of the loud speaker system.

First of all she introduced Boris, their driver for the week, who knew no English but was beginning to pick up a few phrases from the tourists. As they drew away from the airport, Alex began to make her way down the centre of the bus, speaking to everyone in turn, trying to sort out who was who and fit a name to every face before they reached the hotel. On first sight, she had decided that Miss Chandler must be one of the four women who all looked to be in their sixties, but now two were sitting beside men who were undoubtedly husbands, and the other two were the retired schoolteachers.

These two were near the front of the bus, one clutching a guide book. They spoke as if they were seasoned travellers and had read up on the city before leaving home. They won't want to miss a thing, Alex thought. They look reliable, too. Not likely to get lost but if they do, they'll find their way back all right. 'Do you speak any Russian?' she asked encouragingly.

'We've learnt to say 'Good Morning' and 'Thank you' one of them, Miss Trentham, replied with a touch of pride. 'So important to be polite when abroad, I always think. After all, we're ambassadors for Britain, aren't we?'

Behind her, in the front seat reserved for the tour leader, Richard made a sound like a cough. Alex wanted to turn round and glare at him, but decided that would only draw attention, so she ignored it, making a mental note that she'd have a word with him later. If he was likely to offend the clients, Offbeat Tours would see to it that he never continued as one of their tour leaders.

One of the married couples, Mr

and Mrs Balcombe, elderly and rather nervous, had never been anywhere except Benidorm and were branching out a bit, as Mr Balcombe put it. Another, younger couple, Mr and Mrs Banks, the husband looking every inch an executive boss, were prepared to find fault already.

'Speak the lingo, do you?' he demanded brusquely as Alex paused by his seat.

'Yes, I speak Russian. And I'll be with you whenever we go on a scheduled tour — '

'Good,' he snapped. 'Last time we went abroad, wretched guide couldn't speak a word of the language. Hopeless creature.'

'What about the food?' his wife asked anxiously.

'In the hotel, much as you'd find anywhere in Europe. But if you're feeling more adventurous — ' Alex's heart sank as they both recoiled and shuddered. — 'you'll find Russian food a most interesting experience. It's delicious.'

'I don't think so,' the man said coldly.

Why bother to come abroad at all? Alex thought sadly as she moved on.

Her spirits rose as she met the other couples and the mother and daughter, all friendly and pleasant people, all full of enthusiasm and excitement and prepared to enjoy their holiday to the full.

In the last occupied seat was a solitary figure. This had to be Miss Chandler, but Alex's eyes widened in surprise as she reached her. She looked to more than in her early twenties, a rather mouse-like girl, pale faced and nondescript looking.

'Are you Miss Chandler?' Alex asked, unable to keep a trace of surprise out of her voice. 'I thought — '

'Yes, I'm Jane Chandler. I'm travelling alone. Is that a problem?' The girl sounded almost defiant.

'No, no, of course not. It's just that — well, I wasn't expecting someone so young. It's unusual — '

'I don't see why. It seems perfectly reasonable to me to come on a tour like this by one's self. I don't need a friend with me. I wanted to come on my own,' the girl said.

'That's perfectly all right,' Alex replied, smiling encouragingly. 'They look a very friendly group. I'm sure you won't feel lonely at all.'

'I sha'n't be lonely,' Jane Chandler said coldly. Pointedly, she turned her head to stare out of the coach window. A plain, dowdy looking girl, Alex thought, moving back to her seat, though she could do a great deal better for herself if she smiled, or at least looked less grumpy. If she hadn't known from the company notes that Jane had made the single booking originally, Alex would have suspected that she might have been let down by a holiday companion, probably a boyfriend.

They reached the Pribaltiyskaya, enormous, modern and Swedish built; overlooking the Gulf of Finland.

'Typical vast European hotel,' sneered Mr Banks. 'Looks just like any other monster hotel anywhere.'

'I think you'll be very comfortable here,' Alex murmured mildly, ignoring his critical tones. She helped sort out the room allocations at Reception and arranged for the right suitcases to be delivered to the various rooms. She already had her own room here, having arrived the previous day in order to check the final arrangements for the week, before the group arrived.

'I'll leave you to settle in,' she announced, when they had all received their room numbers and an electronic card to open the door. 'We dine together in the restaurant at eight o'clock. The rest of the evening's free; we begin with a tour of the city tomorrow morning.'

She left them to find their own way up to the seventh floor, where they all had been given rooms. Jane, she noticed, had a double room all to herself, having specifically refused to consider sharing with any other single traveller. And there always were enquiries, as Alex knew. She made a mental note to talk to the girl at the first opportunity and find out more about her. The situation and her general manner Alex found intriguing.

The evening meal was veal cutlet and chips, not too unusual as a first experience of food in Russia. She noticed that Mr and Mrs Banks seemed to be enjoying it, though they raised rather supercilious eyebrows at the pot of tea which accompanied it. The two teachers, Miss Trentham and Miss Carson, looked approving. 'Ah, tea! Just what we can do with! How very civilised!' Miss Carson exclaimed with pleasure.

After the meal, several of the group wandered off towards the bar, which doubled as a lounge. Alex was glad to see some seemed to have struck up friendships among themselves already. It made her own job that much easier if the group got on well with each other. She looked round for Jane but did not find her.

Richard came up beside her. 'What would you like to do? Have a nightcap in the bar?'

Alex shook her head. 'I'll give that a miss tonight. They'll ply me with questions and I'd sooner wait until we're on the city tour. Officially, we're off duty now.'

'Well then, would you care to show me my first sight of the Baltic? It's a beautiful night; feels more like early evening than nearly ten o'clock.'

'That's because we're so far north,'

Alex replied. 'Another month and it'll barely get dark at all.'

'Some of the group have gone out for a stroll round, but we can probably avoid them if we're careful,' Richard continued. 'Though they don't seem a bad bunch. Most of them seem sensible, too. Not likely to wander off and lose themselves. The schoolteachers will keep them in order.'

'All right, we'll go to the sea wall and look out over the water, though there's not much to see,' Alex said. 'I wonder, though, if I ought to ask Jane if she'd like to join us? I suspect she may not find it all that easy to make friends.'

'What, plain Jane? Oh, please, not tonight! You said we were officially off duty and she's enough to put a damper on anything. The face of the perennial gooseberry.'

'Richard, that's cruel! The poor girl can't help her looks. It must be sad to have to come on holiday alone. I wonder why she has? I'd like to talk to her and find out more about her.'

15

'But not tonight, please. Anyway, I can't see her anywhere so I suppose she must have gone up to her room.'

'Perhaps those teachers would take her under their wing,' Alex mused. 'Or that nice looking young couple, Mr and Mrs Phillips. They're the only ones anywhere near her age. She really can't have much in common with anyone else. You'll have to be especially nice to her, Richard, so she doesn't feel left out at all.'

'Oh, no!' Richard exclaimed hurriedly. 'I'm not risking anything like that! Being nice to someone got me in trouble before, remember? Even if you've suggested it yourself, if Jane were to get the wrong idea, I'd get the blame, wouldn't I? Just as I did before?'

'That was different. I only thought that if she was lonely by herself — ' Alex floundered.

'Since when has a tour leader's job included escort duties?' Richard snapped. 'Don't try to foist her on me, you'll only get annoyed with me for it later, whatever happens. Don't worry, I'll do my job and see she isn't left out of things, but don't try to make me do anything you might regret later.'

'I'm sorry. I wasn't meaning — I just thought it would be terrible if she spent every evening in her room and never joined in with the others. Perhaps I should go upstairs and see if she's all right — '

'No! She's probably tired after the plane journey. She may be resting and wouldn't appreciate being disturbed. Come on outside and let's look around. You're supposed to be teaching me how to be a good tour leader for St Petersburg, so you really should be showing me the city. We can both start being nice to Jane tomorrow.'

'Very well, then.' It was true Jane wasn't anywhere in sight, and Alex remembered seeing her hurrying out of the dining room towards the lift in a rather purposeful manner, so perhaps she wanted to be on her own for the first evening. She linked her arm through Richard's and together they strolled out of the hotel's main entrance.

At the back of the hotel was a

road, practically traffic-free except for the odd, battered Trabant rattling past, and beyond that was the sea wall. They gazed out at the empty expanse of water, mesmerized by the constant movement of the grey waves.

After some moments, Richard said hesitantly 'You don't mind my being here, do you? They told me they wanted me to take on their Moscow centre in a few months, but I asked if I could go out as an assistant on the St Petersburg tour first, to get the feel of the country.'

'So you asked to come out on this tour?' Alex said. 'I thought you said you were sent.'

'I was sent,' Richard protested. 'They're expecting me to learn a great deal from you. You've more experience as a tour leader in Russia than I have. You're good at dealing with people, too.'

'You can learn that from any tour leader,' Alex said. 'You had the same training by the company as I had, remember? And St Petersburg isn't Moscow. The cities are very different. You'll need a great deal of background study and I can't help you much with that. I've only been to Moscow once.'

'But you're really good at your job. The Director said so.'

'That's not the real reason you asked to come to St Petersburg with my group, is it?' Alex turned to face Richard. 'Look, I think we should get one thing straight. While we're working together — '

'I know,' he broke in. 'I know what you're thinking but it isn't so. I know there's very little chance of us getting back together again.'

'I'm glad you realise that,' Alex said coldly. 'I hoped I'd made it clear.'

'Yes, very clear,' Richard said morosely. 'But surely we can still work together without it affecting our personal lives?'

'Yes, of course we should. Why not? Anyway, I suppose we have to, since you're here.'

'Just tell me one thing.' Richard gazed out across the water, cold and empty, the sun low in the distance. 'Is there anyone else? I mean — I thought — '

Alex shook her head. 'No, there isn't anyone. There never was. I know you thought, when I was on the Majorca tour, that I was interested in one of the tour leaders based there, but, truly, that was nothing more than a professional friendship. But why am I explaining myself to you? Our paths lie in separate directions now. What each of us does is no longer of any concern to the other.'

Richard's mouth tightened into a hard line. 'I suppose not,' he said, after a moment. 'If that's how you see things, then of course I'll try to regard you as a work colleague, nothing more. It'll be hard, after what we once shared, but, as you said, we shouldn't let our personal lives interfere with work.'

Alex took his arm again and drew him away from the wall. 'Look, we shouldn't be talking like this. We have to work together and it would look very bad if any of the group saw us arguing.'

Richard nodded. 'Understood. But isn't it a bit pointless coming to look at the romantic Gulf of Finland if we're keeping each other at arm's length?'

In spite of herself, Alex spluttered with laughter. 'I don't know how an empty expanse of grey sea can possibly look romantic, by any stretch of the imagination,' she said. 'Come on, I'll take you for a stroll round the streets, though it's all appartment blocks round here, nothing much of interest.'

By the time they had crossed the road in front of the Pribaltiyskaya and were heading down a wide street away from the hotel, Richard had recovered his good humour and was practising Russian phrases under Alex's tuition.

Suddenly he broke off. 'Look! Isn't that Jane Chandler ahead?' He pointed to a figure some fifty yards in front, standing by the kerb and about to cross a main road.

'Yes, I think it is! Shall we catch up with her?' Alex quickened her pace. When she judged they were near enough, she called out 'Miss Chandler! Jane! May we join you?'

She couldn't be sure then, but afterwards Alex felt convinced that Jane had heard her, for she appeared to turn her head slightly towards them, then she scurried through a gap in the traffic and disappeared among the pedestrians on the far side of the road.

'Come on, we'll soon catch her up,' Richard said, grabbing Alex's hand. 'She can't have heard us.'

They too, had to wait at the junction for the lights to change and by the time they'd crossed the road Jane was out of sight.

'Where do you think she could be going?' Richard asked. 'As you said, there's nothing much round here except apartment blocks. And she seemed to be walking briskly, as if she had a destination in mind, not merely out for a stroll.'

'Perhaps she always walks like that,' Alex said doubtfully. More and more she was beginning to think that Jane was deliberately avoiding them.

'Has she been to St Petersburg before, do you know? Would she know her way around?' Richard asked.

Alex shook her head. 'I doubt it. Her passport is brand new; I noticed when she registered at Reception. This is the first time she's used it and I wouldn't think she was old enough to be on a renewal yet. Of course, she might have come before with her parents, but she'd have had to be very young not to have had her own passport, even then.'

'She's an oddball,' Richard remarked. 'It seems she doesn't want to be friendly with anyone. I overheard her snubbing the Phillips couple at dinner tonight, when they invited her to join them at their table. You'd think she'd be only too glad to make friends.'

'You get all kinds of people on a package tour like this,' Alex said with a shrug. 'You have to — Look!' she broke off. 'Isn't that her across the road, just about to go into the cemetery?' They had reached the end of the street, which was crossed by another main road, and ahead of them lay an old, gloomy and derelict looking cemetery.

'Why on earth would someone want to go into a place like that?' Richard exclaimed. 'What a depressing place!'

'Oh, I don't know. Some people like wandering round cemeteries. She might like to have someone to translate the

Cyrillic characters on the gravestones for her.'

Jane had slowed her pace now she was in the graveyard. A mud path, made unofficially by many people using the place as a short cut, meandered between the graves, all of which looked very old and neglected.

'Where on earth is she going?' Richard said after a moment. 'She isn't looking at any of the graves or anything.'

Alex dropped back and pulled Richard by the arm. She felt embarrassed to be following Jane, and said so to him.

'It really isn't our business where she goes. She's old enough to take care of herself and she appears quite sensible. Clearly, she doesn't want our company. Let's go back.'

'What is this place?' Richard stopped and began to look around. Silver birch saplings grew in profusion, some tipping gravestones with their roots. Though it was May there were few signs of leaves on the bare twigs.

'It's called the Smolenskoe cemetery. It's huge; there's masses of waste ground

round here. But I don't think she'd get lost.'

'She's met someone,' Richard said. He moved behind a tree and gestured to Alex to come beside him. 'And I thought she didn't know anyone, never been here before.'

'Possibly it's someone trying to sell her something.' There was a worried note in Alex's voice. 'Anyone could tell by her clothes that she's a tourist.'

'I saw some kids sitting on a log, smoking, further back,' Richard said. 'You don't suppose he's a drug dealer, do you?'

'Richard, don't scare me! Perhaps we ought to make sure she's all right.' Alex stepped from behind the tree and walked towards Jane who was some yards ahead, apparently in conversation with a young man. He looked up as Alex approached and drew Jane's attention to her. Jane gave a swift glance in their direction, then hurried away down the path, urging the young man with her.

'Well, that was clear enough,' Richard said. 'She doesn't want us around. Let's go back to the hotel and have ourselves a drink.'

'I suppose she *is* all right,' Alex said doubtfully, staring down the path after Jane and her companion. 'Oh, dear, I've always dreaded something bad happening to one of the group while I'm in charge.'

'She's probably a spy, come to make contact with her control,' Richard teased. Alex's face registered shock.

'Only joking,' he reassured, linking his arm through Alex's and leading her back the way they'd come.

'Don't say things like that! I know the Cold War's over and Russia is very friendly and open now, but I still don't like the idea of spies and neither, I imagine, would the Russian police.'

'I wasn't serious. You must admit, though, that she's behaving very oddly.' Richard strode along the road beside Alex. 'Of course she can't be a spy, or anything like that. Can you imagine anyone employing someone like mousy Miss Chandler as a modern Mata Hari?'

'Richard, this is nothing to joke about. Let's get a drink and sit near the door. I want to have a word with our Jane when she comes in.'

It was about half past eleven when Jane came up the wide flight of steps and entered the hotel lobby. Alex rose from her seat and strolled across to meet her.

'Did you have a pleasant evening?' she enquired casually.

'Yes, thank you,' Jane replied abruptly.

'Would you like a nightcap?' Alex continued. 'They've a good selection at the bar, not just Russian drinks.'

'No, thank you.'

'I didn't realise you knew anyone in St Petersburg,' Alex continued conversationally. 'Have you been here before, then?'

'No. And I don't know anyone here. I mean — ' Jane stopped, aware that Alex had seen her in the cemetery. 'I just spoke to someone.'

'Oh, do you speak Russian, then?' Alex asked innocently.

Jane glared. 'No! But, as I think you said earlier, on the coach, many of the younger Russians know some English.

And if you're thinking of giving me a lecture on not talking to strangers, please don't. I am quite capable of looking after myself.'

'I — I'm sure you are.' Alex was somewhat taken aback by the sharpness of the girl's tone. 'I'll say goodnight,' she mumbled, turning away. 'Don't forget, breakfast is at eight o'clock and the coach leaves at nine-thirty for a tour of the city.'

'I won't forget. Goodnight.' Jane stepped into the lift and the doors closed behind her.

Richard's eyebrows were raised questioningly as Alex returned to him. 'I've been well and truly put in my place,' she said ruefully. 'But, all the same, I'll swear that wasn't a chance conversation she had. It certainly didn't look like it.'

'At least, she came back safely,' Richard said. 'You can't spend all your time playing Nanny to them.'

'I know.' Alex picked up her jacket and turned towards the lift. 'I'm for bed. Busy day tomorrow and you'd better be prepared for them asking lots of questions. They always do.'

Richard nodded. 'I'll be ready. But there are one or two questions I'd like to ask myself, and I'm determined to find out the answers before the end of the week.'

2

The following morning, Alex's group gathered in the hotel foyer after breakfast, ready to board the coach for a tour of the city. Alex noted that when Jane took her place on board, she spread her coat and handbag over the empty seat next to her, a clear hint that she didn't want anyone joining her.

Boris drove them all round the city, with Alex pointing out places of interest and telling them facts and anecdotes about as many of them as she could.

'There's the Winter Palace, better known as the Hermitage museum.' She pointed ahead as they crossed the Dvortsovaya bridge. 'We'll be visiting the Hermitage tomorrow. It's a fantastic place; hundred of rooms and literally millions of exhibits. We'll need to be very selective; it's been calculated that it would take eight years to look, even briefly, at all the exhibits. Unfortunately, we only have a few hours.'

'The highlight of the tour!' cried Miss Carson rapturously. 'I've been longing to see the Hermitage for years!'

'Such beautiful buildings!' exclaimed her friend Miss Trentham. 'Built mostly in the eighteenth century with slave labour, so I've read. How terrible, yet what a monument to man!'

Alex glanced down the coach and saw Jane looking out of the window. She had a bored expression on her face and was fidgeting in her seat as if impatient for the tour to be over.

They stopped at several places during the tour for a closer look at some of the particularly interesting or famous buildings. At the Peter and Paul fortress beside the river they trooped into the church to see the tombs of all the Czars. Soon, the Russian guide informed them, the last Czar, Nicholas, would join his ancestors there, now that they had at last discovered the family's remains from after their assassination.

'How wonderfully well preserved all the churches are!' exclaimed Mrs Phillips. 'I expected them to be mostly in ruins, especially since Russia isn't a very religious country.'

'They look after their historic buildings. They still think of them as national treasures even though the Communists discouraged their use as places of worship,' Alex said. 'And Russians have a great sense of history, even though their history has been very grim at times.'

'All those pretty onion shaped domes!' said Mrs Balcombe excitedly. 'Not a spire or a church tower in sight! How very strange they all look, but so delightful!'

'The onion shape is deliberate,' Alex told them. 'The snow slides off more easily. In fact, it never sticks to that shape so in the midst of the worst snows of winter you can always see the bright gold or coloured stripes of a church dome for miles.'

At lunch time the coach brought them to a side street off the Nevsky Prospekt, the main commercial street of St Petersburg; as famous to Russians as the Champs Elysée or Unter den Linden to western Europeans

'Don't expect to be able to window shop as you would in London,' Alex warned them before they alighted. 'Russians don't display their goods, but you can wander into the shops and look. And there are some cafés where the food is good and very cheap, if you have roubles. The big hotels will take dollars or sterling if you prefer to eat more conventionally. They'll also speak English but you might find the cafés fun and you can always just point to what you want.'

Predictably, most people opted for the large hotel nearby. Alex smiled at Boris and shrugged as she saw him watch the group trail across the side road and enter the hotel.

'I tried, Boris. Really, I tried,' she said to him in Russian. 'People are sometimes very unadventurous when it comes to unfamiliar food.'

'They think they're adventurous even to come and visit this wild and god-forsaken country.' Boris grinned at her. He reached down beside his seat and brought out a packet of sandwiches and a flask. 'I'll stay with the bus. See you back here with your brood in an hour and a half, Alex, my friend.'

'Where are you eating?' Richard was waiting for her outside the coach.

'I know a little place a short way along the Nevsky. The food's delicious and the proprietor and his wife are good friends of mine.'

'Lead on, then! By the end of the week we'll have them all going there and greeting the proprietor in Russian.'

'Some hopes!' Alex laughed. As she left the coach she caught sight of Jane, walking slowly off in the opposite direction from the hotel. Alex quickened her pace and caught up with the girl.

'Where were you planning to eat?' she asked.

Jane looked startled. 'Oh! I — I was going to look inside the shops first. Eat later, perhaps,' she mumbled.

'If you'd like to join Richard and me you'd be more than welcome,' Alex offered.

'No, thank you. I prefer to be on my own,' Jane replied, politely enough but making her wishes abundantly clear.

'Of course. But when you're wanting to find a café — '

'I can read Cyrillic script, thank you. That should ensure I don't get lost, in case you are still worrying about me,' Jane continued frostily. 'And I won't be back late; I'll be at the coach when you want to leave.' She strode off disappearing amongst the crowds in the main street.

'What a pain that girl is!' Richard remarked. 'Just as well the rest of them are so pleasant.'

Alex frowned. 'There's something very odd about her. She wasn't paying attention at any of the places we stopped at, this morning; looked bored and impatient the whole time. I wonder she came at all if she isn't interested. She might have been happier to have spent the week at an English seaside town.'

'She'd have snubbed everyone there, too, I don't doubt,' Richard said. 'Have you noticed that already the others are largely ignoring her? They were all quite friendly at first, but it seems she snubbed all their attempts at being kind to her.

Now it's only those two teachers who speak to her at all. And that's their professional instinct; to befriend the unpopular child in the school.'

Alex's favourite café was down a flight of steps from the street. The front part consisted of a counter with food displayed, a hot plate and two large urns, while the rest of the room consisted of two narrow ledges across the remaining space, where customers could rest plates or glasses while they stood to eat. There were no chairs, but if one wanted to eat in a more leisurely manner, there was a small, inner room beyond, where half a dozen tables and chairs were squashed together. The entrance to this room was through an archway, screened by a curtain made of strips of coloured plastic.

'Hallo, Alex! You have brought the spring with you from London!' Ivan, the proprietor, a huge bear of a man, greeted her warmly. He had an enormous white apron tied round his vast waist and a striped shirt with the sleeves rolled up to show massive, hairy arms. He beamed at them both. 'You've brought one of your

36

little flock to sample Russian food, have you? A success at last!'

Alex smiled and shook her head. 'Not quite. This is Richard. He's another Tour leader, like me. He'll be bringing tourists to Russia, but mainly Moscow.'

'Welcome to St Petersburg, Richard!' Ivan put out a huge, paw-like hand and clasped Richard's own. 'For you both, my best borscht; a speciality of the house! Try this, and then tell your people they won't find better in the whole length of the Nevsky.'

'I'm sure they won't,' Alex said. 'But they seem to be a bit shy of experiencing the real Russian food. One or two might try eventually, but most of them are older people and a bit set in their ways. They prefer to stick to hotel food.'

'Think we are all Russian bears, eh?' Ivan gestured with hands that were indeed like bear paws, and made a ferocious expression.

'Ivan, I know they'd love you if they came here, but perhaps they'd feel embarrassed at not knowing any Russian,' Alex said.

37

'Why should that worry them? I don't know any English and it doesn't worry me!' Ivan gave a great, booming laugh. 'Bring them all with you next time you come this way, little one. They can have the back room to themselves and they needn't see a single Russian except for me. I'll make them very welcome and show them what the Russian people like to eat.'

'I think two of your group have found their way here, Alex.' Maria, Ivan's wife, slipped through the curtain and came round behind the counter. 'There's a couple speaking English in there. Came in a few minutes ago and there aren't many English people in the city these days. It's strange; the man looks Russian but they're certainly speaking a foreign language.'

Alex stepped up to the curtain and parted the plastic strips slightly. Seated at a corner table were Jane and a young man. Alex was sure he was the man they'd seen speaking to Jane in the cemetery yesterday.

'Oh, yes, you're right,' she said

casually, letting the curtain drop. 'She — they — must have come in while we were seeing everyone off the coach. Oh, well, Ivan, where one goes, the rest may eventually follow.'

'I hope so. I can do with the business,' Ivan grinned. 'Why don't you join them? More comfortable than standing.'

'I don't think so. They're — ' While Alex hesitated, trying to think of a way of explaining about Jane, Ivan was quick to grasp what he thought she meant.

'Ah! They are lovebirds, eh? They wish to be by themselves and not disturbed, yes?'

'Something like that,' Alex agreed.

More customers came into the snack bar and Ivan went to serve them.

'What was that all about?' Richard demanded. 'I caught the gist of it, but who is behind that curtain? You seemed very cagey about it.'

'It's Jane,' Alex explained. 'And I'm certain she's with the same chap as we saw her talking to, in the cemetery yesterday.'

'Wow! There must be more to Plain

39

Jane than we thought,' Richard remarked. 'Only here less than two days and she's found herself a Russian boyfriend! How does she do it?'

Alex frowned. 'Don't joke, please, Richard. I don't like the situation. I feel there's something fishy about the whole thing. If she's friendly enough with the chap to meet him for lunch, why did she pretend she didn't know him?'

'I said she was a spy,' Richard said. 'The Cold War may be over, but I bet there's still plenty of cloak and dagger stuff still going on. This tour would be perfect cover — '

'No, it wouldn't,' Alex disagreed. 'It would be hopeless. Well, aren't we suspicious of her already? But you're living in fantasy land, Richard. Spies don't look like Jane Chandler, and at the very least they know the language of the country they're spying in. Jane doesn't know much more than the Russian alphabet.'

'How do you know that? Only because she told you. And she would, wouldn't she? She wouldn't want to draw attention to it if she could speak Russian.'

'I simply cannot believe anything so far-fetched,' Alex said impatiently. 'You just don't have spies on a package tour. It's ridiculous.'

'But you admit there's something odd about her?' Richard persisted. 'Why don't we challenge her now, ask her outright who this chap is. You've a right to. You're in charge of the group and if she was doing anything that might cause trouble, the rest of the group could be put at risk.'

'This would have to happen!' Alex sighed. 'It's worse than someone falling ill or breaking a leg. There are company rules for dealing with things like that.'

'Tell you what,' Richard's eyes lit up as an idea came to him, 'I'll see them safely through the rest of today's tour. Boris knows where we're going and I can get him to tell me something about the buildings we pass — you follow the man Jane's with and see what you can find out about him. Chat him up, or try to find out who he is. Find out where he lives.'

'I don't know.' Alex considered the idea. 'This isn't like England. If he wanted to cause trouble it might become rather awkward. The Russians are a great deal less suspicious of foreigners than they used to be, but they still are a bit wary.'

Richard moved to take a look through the curtain between the two rooms. 'You'll have to make up your mind quickly. Jane's standing up; they'll be leaving soon.'

'Let's get out of here.' Alex grabbed Richard's arm and dragged him up the steps to the street. They were strolling back towards the coach when Jane passed them, returning in good time as she'd promised.

Alex gave her a warm smile. 'You were more adventurous than the others, eating in a Russian snack bar,' she said. 'Have you had Russian food before?'

Her tone was casual, the comment conventional. She was unprepared for the angry response. 'It's none of your business where or what I eat! I do wish you wouldn't continually snoop on me!'

42

'I'm sorry!' Alex gasped. 'I wasn't — I mean, I always eat at Ivan's café when I'm here; I didn't know you were there when I went in. I wasn't snooping at all.'

It was Jane's turn to look abashed. 'Sorry,' she muttered. 'I thought — well, you keep asking me if I'm all right and I'm not a child. I'm quite capable of looking after myself. I don't need a nursemaid. And I like my own company; I prefer it.'

But you haven't been having your own company, Alex thought but resisted speaking out loud. She made up her mind. 'Oh, Richard, see them all back into the coach for me, will you?' she said. 'I want to buy some fruit. I'll catch you up at one of the sightseeing stops. Don't wait for me. Tell Boris to drive on and keep to the schedule.' She turned back and began walking towards the main street again.

Jane started after her with a doubtful look on her face, but Richard, thinking quickly, took her by the arm and, steering her towards the waiting coach, said 'come

43

and tell me what you think of the Russian doll I bought this morning. Well, six dolls actually, one inside the other. From a street trader outside the hotel. Did you see them? They have all kinds of carvings and painted things. The back streets must be full of people churning out tourist junk to sell, I should think.' Chattering to her, he helped Jane on to the coach. Alex had evidently decided to act on his suggestion; what she was going to do he didn't know, but with luck she'd find out something about this mysterious friend of Jane's. He didn't expect to see her for some time, and told Boris to drive off as soon as everyone was settled in the coach.

Alex turned the corner into the Nevsky Prospekt and was relieved to see the young man just coming out of Ivan's café. She hadn't yet decided what she would do. If she spoke to him, what should she say? There was no law forbidding Russians from speaking to foreigners but there had been times in the past when such a thing might have drawn unwelcome attention on the

Russian and perhaps some of them were still a bit cautious. This man might think she was accusing him of something, but, anyway, what right had she to question him about his actions?

All the same, she *was* curious about him. She found herself following him as he walked down Nevsky Prospekt towards the far end, away from where the coach had been. He looked about twenty three or four, a year or so older than Jane, she surmised, and appeared to be Russian, though he wore jeans and a leather jacket, the international uniform of the young.

After about a hundred yards or so, he stopped at a bus stop. Alex stopped as well, trying to think of a way of starting a conversation that would seem natural and unthreatening to him.

'Excuse me,' she said at last, in English, 'but can you tell me if the bus — '

He shook his head. 'I'm sorry. I speak only Russian,' he said in that language.

Alex could hardly begin again and show that she was fluent in his language, but she was so startled that she couldn't have thought of anything further to say, anyway. She was sure Jane didn't know Russian; and Maria had said they were speaking English in the café and Maria knew what English sounded like, even if she didn't know any herself.

While she was still puzzling what to do next, a bus arrived. Alex followed Jane's mystery man inside and sat as far to the back as possible so that she could observe him. The fare was a flat rate of five kopeks so she had no problem about stating a destination.

The journey lasted long enough for Alex to begin worrying about what she was doing. Richard could cope with the group, no problems there, but it wasn't very professional or responsible of her to slip away and leave them, to follow a stranger to Heaven knew where, in the city.

She had almost decided to get out at the next stop and take a bus back, whatever happened, when the man stood up and began to make his way towards the exit. Alex had been half out of her seat before he'd moved, so it didn't appear that she was following him. On the pavement she looked around, then fumbled in her handbag for the street map she always carried. It didn't seem to show streets this far out of the city centre, although they couldn't have come much further than a mile from the end of Nevsky Prospekt. This was a residential area, the inevitable tower blocks of apartments on either side. Only the very rich or highly placed officials lived in houses in St Petersburg.

While she was turning the pages of her street map, the man strode off purposefully down the street. She'd come this far, Alex thought, she might as well see where the man lived, even though she could hardly start up any conversation with him now.

He turned a corner and entered a side door of the first apartment block on his left. It was some twenty storeys high and there was no way of telling which floor he could have been making for. There were probably several apartments on each floor anyway. Alex berated herself for her stupidity. She might have known that he would live somewhere in an anonymous block of apartments and there was no means of finding out where without him being aware of her following him. This silly jaunt had gained her nothing and now she was in an unfamiliar part of the city and would have to find her way back somehow. But the mystery of the man's connection with Jane, still persisted in her thoughts, and not least because of Jane's strangely defensive manner.

Alex arrived back at the Pribaltiyskya hotel shortly before her group returned from their afternoon excursion.

'Everything go all right?' she greeted Richard. 'No problems?'

'Look, I'm not a complete idiot. I can manage to take a group of tourists round a city without creating a disaster,' he complained. 'How about you?'

'Sorry, Richard. I know you're just as competent as I am. More so, in fact. I'm the one who's been the complete idiot.' She told him briefly of her bus trip following Jane's mystery man.

'Don't look upon it as entirely a waste of time,' Richard comforted. 'At least, now we know roughly where he lives You didn't manage to speak to him?'

'He claimed not to know any English. If that's true, Jane is pretending not to know any Russian.'

'I know, I'll get one of the waiters, at dinner tonight, to tell her she's dropped her purse, or something. If she reacts without realising, then we'll know.'

'Richard, this is awful. We're treating our clients as if they were, well, somehow not to be trusted. We can't keep checking on them like this.'

'We don't know if Jane is to be trusted,' Richard said reasonably. 'She's been acting very strangely and we have a right to find out why. She could be involved with drugs or currency dealings. She could be putting the safety of the rest of the group at risk. We cannot allow that.'

'I simply can't believe anything like that of Jane! It must be someone she's met, something perfectly innocent — '

'How could she have met him? I'll swear he wasn't on the plane with us, yet she had a rendezvous with him on our first evening. She didn't have time to meet him before then. And he's acting oddly, too, not admitting he knows any English. We know he speaks it; Maria heard him.'

'Richard, I'm so glad you're here to share the problem with me,' Alex said impulsively.

'Glad to be of some use,' Richard replied lightly. Then, more seriously, he added 'you know that I'll always be there for you, whenever you need me. I don't mean just this week, but any time. If, in the future — '

'Thank you, Richard,' Alex said coolly. 'I'll be grateful for your *professional* help while we're here, but as to anything in general — '

'I mean it, Alex.'

'I'm sure I can always count on you as a friend and colleague,' Alex finished briskly. She turned away. She didn't want to see the hurt expression in Richard's eyes. Bother him! He had no right to be hurt because she was keeping him at arm's length. When they had met on the training course Offbeat Tours ran for all their fledgling tour leaders, Richard had seemed so different from anyone she had met before; he had been special to her, and she'd had every reason to think that the feeling was mutual. Then she'd discovered that he had been seeing someone else and hadn't been honest enough to tell her about it. Alex had been hurt but had consoled herself with the thought that she would have little time to grieve over a lost love. She would be doing what she enjoyed most, travelling to interesting and exciting places, learning all about them and helping other people to discover how interesting and exciting they were, too. She had assumed that Richard would be assigned to somewhere far away; Offbeat Tours ran holidays to the Far East and South America, too, so it had been something of a shock to discover that Richard, too, was to be a tour leader for some of the Russian tours. So far, he had not taken a group to Russia on his own, though he was scheduled to do so soon. Alex walked into the hotel restaurant for dinner, determined not to let her feelings interfere with her job.

Richard was a colleague, a work friend. She must try to think of him like that, and as nothing more than that.

The following morning they set off for what was considered by many of the group to be the highlight of the whole week, the visit to the Hermitage museum, in the old Winter Palace facing out over the Neva river. There were reputed to be an incredible eight million objects housed in the museum, everything from exquisite jewellery to works of art representing all the schools of Europe. Alex had visited the Hermitage several times, never failing to have her breath taken away by the sheer beauty and workmanship of the exhibits. She also never failed to lose herself among the thousands of rooms and hundreds of staircases comprising the fabulous building. She had, therefore, organised an English speaking Russian guide to escort the group round and she found she was looking forward to the visit as much as any of them, none of whom had any real idea of the extent of the treasures they were about to see.

The coach trundled over the Dvortsovaya

bridge and the Hermitage stretched in front of them. They were to park behind the building, in the enormous square of the same name, with the Alexander Column at its centre.

Glancing back down the coach, Alex noticed Jane fanning her face furiously with a pamphlet. When they stopped, she said faintly to Alex 'Oh, Alex, do you mind if I don't go into the museum? I feel so rotten. I think I'm developing a migraine.'

Immediately there was sympathy and concern from everyone on the coach. 'But you simply *can't* miss the Hermitage!' said Miss Trentham, scandalised. 'It's a once in a lifetime experience!' Mrs Balcombe proffered aspirin and smelling salts.

'No, thank you,' Jane whispered pathetically. 'They never have any effect when I'm like this. I couldn't manage going round anywhere. All I want to do is lie down in a darkened room. Do you think Boris would take me back to the hotel? Would that be terribly inconvenient?' She looked so wan that Alex forgot how difficult Jane had been in the last few days. 'No, that will be perfectly all right. Boris can drive you back, if that's what you'd prefer, and he'll be back in plenty of time to pick us up. Are you sure I can't get you anything for it, though? The chemists here stock everything you could need.'

'No, thank you. I have some pills in my room. All I need is to lie down for a few hours. But I feel so dizzy — I couldn't possibly walk very far anywhere,' Jane whispered.

Alex looked at her anxiously. 'Shall I come back with you? Richard can see to the guide; it doesn't need two of us here. Perhaps the hotel could find you a doctor?' The girl really did look unwell, her face flushed and her body shivering. No, no, please don't let her have caught some dreadful illness, Alex begged silently. She knew what the company instructions were in such cases but it was one thing knowing in theory, quite another to be faced with such an emergency in fact.

'Please don't let me spoil your day.

I'll be all right, really.' Jane sounded genuinely concerned. 'All I need is some undisturbed rest in my room and I'll be feeling better by tomorrow.'

'At least let me come back with you,' Alex urged.

'I wouldn't dream of it. Boris can take me back to the hotel. That's all I need. I shouldn't have come today but I felt all right earlier.'

Slowly, the rest of the group filed out of the coach. There were many sympathetic looks and murmured comments as they went. The group had gelled into a close-knit, friendly band now, and although they found Jane unresponsive to their approaches, they were a kindly bunch, most of them old enough to regard their youngest member with something like parental concern.

Briefly, Alex explained the situation to Boris. 'Just see she gets up the steps safely and isn't bothered by any of the touts selling things outside,' she said. 'I should think it's as she says; once she can rest in her room for a while, she'll feel better. I certainly hope so; I don't want her coming down with something serious.'

'I'll be back within the hour, long before they'll want to leave here,' Boris assured her. 'Don't worry, Alex, I'll keep an eye on her and see she gets back to the hotel safely.'

As soon as they had all alighted and were trailing across the square towards the Hermitage entrance, he started the engine and headed back towards the bridge.

The Hermitage, as Alex knew it would, lived up to and even excelled everyone's expectations. They lingered over the superb examples of furniture, sculpture, coins, porcelain and jewellery. Alex knew they could never hope to see a hundredth of what was on display.

'Like eating a banquet of strawberries and cream!' Miss Carson exclaimed. 'It's simply all too much to take in! And such a wonderful setting! The rooms are redolent of history.'

Outside the museum Alex found Boris waiting for her. 'Miss Chandler managed to reach the hotel without mishap, did she?' She asked him.

Boris made a face. 'Said she had a bad headache, did she? Well, it didn't look to me as if there was much wrong with her. If she was ill, she made a miraculous recovery.'

'What do you mean?' Alex asked.

'I took her back to the hotel, as you said. She just thanked me in English when she got off and I watched her go up the steps to the entrance. I had to pull round the corner then as there was another coach bringing more tourists to the hotel, and I was waiting to pull out and come back here when I saw her come down the steps again, not five minutes later. She didn't notice me but I saw her all right. I could hardly believe my eyes when she scuttled off down the road as if she was going off somewhere. I thought you said she felt too dizzy to walk anywhere? To me, she looked perfectly well.'

'What on earth is she playing at!' Alex exclaimed angrily. 'And everyone was so kind and sympathetic to her, too!'

Boris shrugged philosophically. 'All

the time, all I hear from tourists is Hermitage, Hermitage. Perhaps this one didn't want to see our national treasures. It's possible.'

'Boris, anything's possible,' Alex sighed. She saw them all back into the coach and then went to speak to Richard privately outside before they drove off.

'What did she want to do that for?' Richard exploded. 'That girl's a thorough liability! She caused you worry, thinking she was really ill.'

'I don't know what she's up to, but this time I mean to find out,' Alex said. 'I'm having no more of these mysterious meetings with a strange Russian man. I know she's not a child, but I am responsible for everyone on the tour and I think I have a right to be told what's going on. I intend to demand an explanation as soon as I see her again.'

3

On their return to the hotel, Alex went up to Jane's room and knocked on the door. There was no sound from within.

'I expect she's still sleeping it off, poor lamb,' said Mrs Balcombe, passing on her way to her own room. 'It's awful to be unwell on holiday. I do feel so sorry for the poor child.'

Alex resisted the urge to inform her that Jane was undeserving of sympathy. She merely nodded and lingered in the corridor until Mrs Balcombe had gone into her own room.

There was a housekeeper's room at the end of the corridor and, fortunately, two chambermaids working inside, sorting linen. Alex explained that she was concerned about one of the group who was unwell, and one of the maids willingly came back with her to unlock the door with her passkey.

Jane's room was empty and her bed

showed no evidence that anyone had even laid down on it for a moment.

'She must have felt better and gone out for some fresh air,' Alex explained. The maid, incurious, went back to her work, and Alex went to find Richard.

Jane did not put in an appearance at dinner time. There were several enquiries after her, which Alex parried by replying that Jane must be still sleeping her headache off.

'Quite right. You don't want food if you're not feeling well,' Mrs Banks agreed. 'Especially food that's a bit different from what you're used to. Though I must say, what we're having tonight is absolutely delicious.'

After dinner, Alex and Richard bought drinks from the bar and took them to seats near the hotel entrance. The rest of the group were off to see the Leningrad State Circus, so this was an ideal opportunity to speak to Jane privately. That is, Alex thought anxiously, if the girl was going to reappear at all.

At half past ten, Jane came in through the glass doors. She was clutching a large, flat parcel, wrapped in garish paper, to her chest. She looked round warily and was about to make for the lifts when Alex and Richard, together, stood up and blocked her way.

'Hallo, Jane! Your migraine seems to have improved miraculously!' Alex greeted her. 'I heard it seemed to get better as soon as you arrived back here. I'm *so* glad!'

Jane looked guilty. 'Yes, I do feel much better now. The fresh air must have done me good.' She tried to pass them but Richard neatly side-stepped and blocked her way.

'We thought we'd wait here for you because we'd like a little chat with you,' Alex said. 'The others are at the circus so we won't be interrupted. Care for a drink, perhaps?'

Jane looked as if she could do with a drink, but she shook her head. 'No, thanks. Look, I really am rather tired. Perhaps we could talk another time?'

'I'm afraid not,' Richard said, taking her arm and steering her towards one of the seats. 'We need to talk to you now.'

He sat down facing her and said 'I'm going to be blunt. Alex is responsible for the safety of everyone on this tour. She's worried about you. You go wandering off, goodness knows where, and you tell lies about it. It's just not on. Russia isn't like France or Germany; you could get yourself into difficulties and the Russian police can be awkward people to deal with, especially if they think there may be something funny going on.'

'What do you mean, something funny going on?' Jane demanded. She glared at him defiantly and Alex's heart sank. The girl was going to be difficult and really, they had no right to question her like this, anyway.

'I mean, if they think you might be doing some illegal currency deals with a Russian national,' Richard said bluntly.

Shock, and a look of fear, registered on Jane's face.

'I wasn't doing anything like that! Really I wasn't!'

'I'm very relieved to hear it,' Alex broke in, before Richard could continue. 'So, what were you doing? You were seen speaking to a Russian man on more than one occasion, yet you say you have never been to Russia before and don't know anyone here. If that man is a stranger it could be dangerous, and not only to you. He might find himself in trouble with the police if you keep seeing him in such a secretive, suspicious way.'

'I wasn't doing anything wrong!' Jane insisted, though she looked rather scared. She clutched her parcel even more tightly to her chest. 'It isn't anything like what you think. It wasn't a pick-up; he's not a stranger. I know him.'

'You know him? How?' Richard asked in surprise.

'He — he's a pen friend. I've been writing to him for more than six months. That's why I wanted to come on this trip. I'm not really interested in museums or palaces or anything like that but I wanted to meet him. He lives in St Petersburg.'

'A pen friend!' Alex gasped. 'But why didn't you say so earlier? he could have joined us on the coach if he liked; there's plenty of room.'

'No. He wouldn't have wanted that. Neither would I.'

'At least you must invite him here to the hotel. He could have dinner with us one evening. I'm sure the rest of the group would love to meet a real Russian who can answer all their questions about life here.'

Jane shook her head. 'He wouldn't come. Look, I just came on this trip to meet him. I'm not in any danger from him so you don't have to worry about me.' She added 'My father knows about him; *he* thought I'd be all right.'

'Well, if he's a friend and you know him, that's all right,' Alex said. 'But why were you so secretive about it? Why didn't you tell us at the beginning that you'd come to visit your friend? I wouldn't have been so concerned about you if I'd known.'

Jane hesitated just a fraction too long before answering. 'I thought you'd insist that I joined in with all the excursions,' she said lamely.

'What's this chap's name?' Richard asked. 'We can't go on calling him

Jane's mystery man.'

A ghost of a smile passed Jane's lips. 'Is that what you've been calling him? His name's Mikhail Levchenko. He works in a furniture maker's yard outside the city. But you won't have to worry about me any more after today. Mikhail's having to be at work for the rest of the week, so I won't be seeing him again.'

'He seems to have given you a nice parting gift,' Richard observed, gesturing towards the parcel. 'What is it, a book about St Petersburg?'

Jane's grip on the parcel tightened. 'No. Er — well, I suppose it could be. I — er, I'm not sure. Look, I really am tired. If you've finished your interrogation I should like to go up to my room.'

The group had returned from the circus and were starting to come in through the main doors into the marble floored entrance hall. They were talking excitedly, clearly having enjoyed the performance enormously. Alex realised that if they saw Jane they'd all begin telling her what she'd missed, asking her if she still felt unwell, plying her with awkward questions.

'You go now, before the others notice you're here.' She gave Jane a little push towards the lifts. Jane took a couple of paces, then turned back. 'Alex — I really am sorry if I caused you to worry about me,' she mumbled. For a moment, she looked about ten years old.

'That's all right. I'm just relieved to know what the situation is. Now, get to the lifts before they see you.' Alex was touched by the girl's apparent vulnerability.

As soon as she'd gone, Richard picked up his glass and drained it. 'Pen friend my foot!' he snorted. 'You don't believe that, do you?'

'It's possible, I suppose. It would explain how she came to know him.'

'If it was as simple as that, she'd have told you at the beginning. And she wouldn't have been so secretive about it. Believe me, there's more to this than she's told us.'

'Whatever it was, it looks as if she won't be going off to meet him again,' Alex said. 'I only hope that doesn't mean we're going to have a moody, lovesick girl on the coach for the last two days.'

Several of the group had now seen them and came over, drinks in hand, to enthuse about the circus.

'Wonderful!' said Mr Phillips. 'The acrobats were the best I've ever seen. You'd never believe a human body could do things like that.'

For once, the critical Mr Banks had no fault to find. 'They had a troupe of performing Afghan hounds,' he said in awed tones. 'I had an Afghan for years and I couldn't manage to teach it anything, not even to come when it was called. They're supposed to be untrainable, like cats, but the trainer had them doing amazing things.'

'Must have taken *hours* to groom them all,' his wife added feelingly.

The last two days of the tour were packed with action but free from stress for Alex. They visited Petrodvorets, the summer palace of Peter the Great, with its incredible flight of fountains across gardens reminiscent of Versailles. They visited Pushkin, a small town outside

St Petersburg where the last Czar and his family had lived for some months after the Revolution. Jane, though she appeared quiet and rather wrapped in her own thoughts, joined in every trip and stayed with the rest of the group. She parried the kindly meant enquiries about her migraine and even joined in some of the conversation. The others were all firm friends now, on the final day exchanging addresses and promises of sending copies of snapshots to each other. The last day they had an evening of Russian folk dancing and a special farewell dinner.

'Jane, why don't you invite your friend to join us this evening?' Alex asked her in the afternoon. 'He surely can't be working all the time. It would be nice to say goodbye to him at a party, wouldn't it?'

'He wouldn't come,' Jane said abruptly.

'Surely he couldn't be shy — and he speaks English quite well, doesn't he?'

'Yes, very well. He needs to; I don't know any Russian,' Jane said. 'But we've said our goodbyes and, like I said, he wouldn't want to come.'

Alex said no more, but Richard, who had overheard the conversation, muttered 'Perhaps they've quarrelled. Or, as I suspected all along, he isn't a pen friend at all but someone more sinister.'

'I know your mind is still running on thoughts of currency rackets or drugs,' Alex said. 'But not Jane! Who'd choose her if they were looking for someone for that kind of thing? She's far too naive, and I'm sure she hasn't enough money to be of interest to a crook.'

'We'll be rid of her by tomorrow afternoon,' Richard said. 'I don't suppose we'll ever see or hear of her again after that. Can't say I'll be sorry, but we've been lucky with the rest of the group.'

Boris arrived with the coach after breakfast to drive them to the airport. Richard was returning to London but Alex had another group arriving that evening so she was staying on at the Pribaltiyskaya. They'd been late finally getting to bed that last evening. The Russian entertainment had turned into a group party, and after most of the guests had retired to bed, Alex and Richard had stayed on in the bar, talking.

'We managed to survive a week of working together without a battle,' Richard said, bringing her a drink. 'So, are we friends again, now?'

'Why shouldn't we be friends?' Alex accepted the drink but she didn't smile at him.

'I meant, am I forgiven for whatever it was I did to upset you?'

Alex set her glass down. 'You don't even know what you did, do you?' she said.

'No, I don't. All I know is that, somehow, I upset you. We were getting along very well together, or so I thought, and then, suddenly, you were annoyed with me. I never knew why. You wouldn't speak to me, or tell me what was wrong. I was completely baffled.'

Alex twisted the glass between her fingers. She didn't speak for a few moments, then said 'So you don't think going out with another girl behind my back was a reason for me to be upset, or annoyed with you?'

'Going out with another girl behind

your back? What's that supposed to mean?' Richard was looking genuinely puzzled.

'Are you saying then, that you didn't go out with Caroline Roberts? As I understood it, you and she went to Bristol for the weekend. Isn't that true?'

Richard's jaw tightened. 'I wonder who your obliging informant was. Yes, it's true I took Caroline to Bristol and it was while you were away on that course in Majorca. And yes, I did stay overnight. At her home, in fact.'

'And you didn't think of mentioning it to me?'

'You weren't there to tell. As I said, it was while you were in Majorca. By the time you came back — well, I was going to tell you but it seemed someone else got word in first.'

'And you thought it wouldn't matter? That I wouldn't mind?'

'Frankly, no. It didn't occur to me that I needed your permission to take Caroline to Bristol. She lives there, you know.'

'I thought,' Alex said slowly 'that we

had something special going between us in those days. Something I thought included trust.'

'I thought so, too,' Richard said with some bitterness. 'But it seems you didn't trust *me*. And I was fool enough to think I could be sure of your understanding.'

'Understanding!' Alex exclaimed. 'If we'd merely been friends, or if you'd known Caroline before me, there might be some excuse, but you — you let me down, Richard, going off with her as soon as I'd left for Majorca.'

'If that's how you saw the situation I haven't anything more to say,' Richard replied coldly. 'I'm not going to explain or try to justify myself. You probably wouldn't believe me, anyway. You'd sooner believe some gossip monger who wanted to stir up trouble between us.'

'You said it was true. So it wasn't mere gossip,' Alex pointed out.

'Yes, it was true. I spent the entire weekend with Caroline. And I'm not discussing it any further. If that's a problem to you, then I'm sorry.'

'I thought part of it might have been

that you were jealous of Phillip Farrer. That you were getting your own back,' Alex said.

'Phillip? Why should I be jealous of him?' Richard's eyebrows shot up in surprise. 'What's Phillip got to do with it?'

'He was based in Majorca when I was out there. He's always been rather fond of me, and I thought — '

'You thought I didn't trust you?' Richard said. 'You thought I'd assume the worst, and would retaliate in kind. What a low opinion you must have of me.'

'I'm sorry, Richard. I didn't think that at first, and you must realise that nothing happened between Phil and me, either then or at any other time — '

'That's no concern of mine, now,' Richard said harshly. 'We're free agents, both of us. But surely we can still be friends, as well as colleagues? We've proved it's possible; we haven't come to blows yet and we've worked together the best part of the week.'

'Yes, and that's a relief,' Alex confessed.

'When I realised you were to be here as well I thought things might become very difficult.'

'A bit like walking on eggshells?' Richard suggested. His tone softened. 'I've felt like that with you sometimes this week. It was the great drama of our mysterious Jane that was the one thing that kept us behaving normally towards each other. She may have been a nuisance, but you've got that to thank her for.'

'And tomorrow she'll be gone.'

'And so will I. It's a shame we wasted this week keeping each other at arm's length and now we won't see each other for a further week. When you get back next Sunday, may I meet you at the airport and take you out to dinner? No strings attached, I promise, but I expect you'll be quite glad of some British cooking by then.'

'I'd like that.' Alex smiled at him. 'Provided you're not off on another assignment. The holiday season is well underway now, we might keep missing each other from now till October.'

'I'll see I'm there, even if I have to call in sick and join my tour late,' Richard promised. 'And now, I think we'd better go up to our rooms. The barman is giving us anxious looks. He wants to close up and get to bed himself.'

Outside her door, Richard took Alex's hand, drawing her towards him. She did not resist as his arm slid round her shoulders and his lips touched her own, lightly. Her heart ached; Richard wanted to be friends but he didn't seem to want more than that. So much she wished that the weekend with Caroline had never happened! If only they could have spent this week as they had once been, during that heady, glorious time when they had been training together.

'Richard — ' She broke free to speak.

'We're friends now. Leave it like that. No commitments. We don't have to explain anything to each other.'

Her heart sank at his words. He seemed to be telling her very clearly that Caroline was still part of his life and he had no intention of changing that. That Alex herself was not important enough for him to make any serious commitment to her.

'Richard, I'll come to the airport to see you all off tomorrow,' she said with an effort. 'And if you were to meet me off the plane next week, I'd be delighted. But only if you haven't any other commitments.'

'I'll be there,' Richard said, releasing her. Without a backward glance he continued on down the corridor to his own room.

Next morning, they piled into Boris's coach for the last time, for the journey to the airport. Everyone was a little subdued, a good sign that they had all enjoyed their week in St Petersburg, Alex decided. She looked over to where Jane was sitting, by herself as usual. She wondered if her pen friend would manage to come to the airport to see her off; it seemed to have been a rather abrupt ending to their brief acquaintance.

It took nearly an hour to drive to Pulkovo, south of the city, where the airport was situated. They had, of course, to check in some time before their flight was called and most had planned to spend the rest of their currency in the duty free shop, and eating lunch in the airport café.

Alex stayed with them until it was time for them to go through the customs barrier, then she began saying goodbye to each of them in turn. She found it quite a wrench; realising she had come to know and like them all in the week they'd been together, and after today she would probably never see any of them again.

'Come travelling with Offbeat Tours again,' she said, clasping Miss Trentham's wrinkled hand.

'Oh, we will, dear! We certainly will!' Miss Carson cried. 'And we'll ask particularly when you are going to be the tour leader. Goodbye, dear. I'm sure we shall see you again before very long.'

Alex turned away and was startled to see Jane staring at her, a look of consternation on her face.

'Why are you saying goodbye here?' Jane demanded.

'I'm not going on the plane with you.

I have a group of businessmen arriving this evening who need escorting round the city,' Alex explained.

'But you must come back with us!' Jane gasped. 'Surely you have to escort us back to London!'

Alex laughed. 'You'll be perfectly all right. You don't need me. And Richard is flying back with you. He can give you any help you may need at Heathrow.'

Jane shook her head, her eyes filling with tears. 'This is awful,' she whispered. 'I — I think I'd better not go on this flight after all — '

'I'm afraid you'll have to,' Alex said briskly. 'We can't change tickets now. You'll have to go with the group. Look, you can write to your pen friend and perhaps he might be able to come to England — ' She hesitated, aware that though Russians were allowed to travel to the west, the high costs involved made it virtually impossible for most of them.

'It's not that!' Jane said impatiently. 'Look, I simply *have* to get back to the hotel. It's important — '

'Sorry, Jane. Our flight has been called.'

Richard took her by the arm. 'Bye, Alex! See you at Heathrow in a week!'

Jane resisted his grasp and tried to come back through the turnstile type barriers, without success. 'Alex! Get me back!' she screamed.

Two uniformed officials stepped forward, bearing down on her. One took her hand luggage, the other a firm grip on her arm. 'This way, Madame,' he announced, steering her towards the gate leading to departures. Though they were both perfectly polite, there was an air of authority about them which it was impossible to resist. Alex's last sight of Jane was the girl being marched briskly out of sight through the departure gate.

With a last wave to them all, Alex made her way out to the car park. Boris was in high spirits. 'So generous with their tips, and almost all in hard currency!' he chortled. 'Bring another nice group like that, Alex, please.'

'The next ones will be more serious. They're looking to investigate business opportunities in the city,' Alex told him.

'We'll be taking them mainly to offices and factories.'

'But they must have some entertainment in the evening,' Boris said. 'They can't work all the time. And they must see something of my beautiful city.'

'They will, Boris. I'll make sure they do,' Alex promised. 'Now, take me back to the hotel, will you please? We have precisely eight hours free before you drive me back again to meet their plane.'

At the hotel, the receptionist called to her: 'Miss Vincent, one moment, if you please.'

The young man behind the desk looked apologetic. 'I'm so sorry, Miss Vincent, but I have to ask you to move your room on to the fourth floor. We're putting your party where there is a business suite for them to use; fax, photocopying facilities and so on. Your company asked for this since I understand they are here for trade purposes.'

'Yes, that's right. I don't mind changing my room at all,' Alex said. 'I'll do it straight away.'

'One of the chambermaids could do it

for you. No problem.'

'No, I can easily do it myself. Just give me the new room pass and I'll go up now.'

Pleased that Alex had accepted the change of room without complaint, the receptionist smiled as he handed her the credit card sized plastic pass, which was programmed to open the door of her new room. He had come to know Alex over the last year, when she had brought several groups of tourists to the Pribaltiyskaya, and he had always found her pleasant and co-operative, a very likeable woman. Although his English was good, he appreciated the fact that she spoke Russian to all the staff; so many of the British or American visitors made no effort over using the Russian language.

Alex went upstairs to her old room and dragged her suitcase from the bottom of the cupboard. She dumped it on the bed and threw back the lid. There were still a few things inside that she hadn't unpacked and she was about to pile clothes on top, when she stopped, frowning in puzzlement. There was something in the suitcase which certainly hadn't been there before. In the bottom lay a large, flat package wrapped in the patterned paper that shops frequently used. Before she had even lifted it out, she guessed what it was. It was the package she had last seen Jane clutching to her chest as she came into the hotel a few evenings ago.

What on earth is it doing in my suitcase? Alex thought. Then, oh, dear, Jane must have intended it as a present for me! A thank you and perhaps some sort of apology for being an awkward tourist. She was touched, but still a little puzzled. Why hadn't Jane given it to her personally? Why had she gone to the trouble of leaving it for her to find in her suitcase? There was something faintly annoying in the fact that the girl must somehow have got into her room without Alex's knowledge, to leave the present.

Was this somehow an explanation of Jane's odd behaviour at the airport? If Alex had been leaving with the group, she would have packed her case and presumably found the package, though possibly not, since it had been underneath some clothes and a dress which Alex had not unpacked on this trip.

I suppose I'd better see what she's given me, Alex thought, pulling at an edge of the paper. Perhaps there's some note with it which will explain things a bit more fully. It's probably a book on Russia, or maybe one of the sketches the street artists are always trying to sell to tourists. I don't think I need anything like that, but I suppose it's a kind thought —

The paper fell away and Alex's jaw dropped in astonishment. It *was* a picture, but not one any street artist would have offered for sale. It was an icon, a Russian religious picture, but this was no ordinary one. The base was of wood, hard as ebony and blackened with age, but covered with beaten silver on one side. The head of the Virgin was etched in the silver, and she and the Infant's head bore haloes of gold, each inlaid with minute diamonds. The picture itself was decorated with precious stones of all kinds, the robes of the figures being covered with them. The icon was clearly very old, and also undoubtedly very, very valuable. This was no mere thank you gift, this was of the order of a national treasure.

Alex turned over the wrapping paper but there was no note of explanation, nothing with it to indicate the reason it had been put in her suitcase. She remembered how Jane had come into the hotel, clutching the package nervously to her chest and avoiding Richard's curious comments. She stared at the picture, mesmerized by it. It was beautiful, but how on earth had Jane come into possession of such an object? Was it possible that she had stolen it from one of the museums, one of the great churches or the Hermitage itself, perhaps? It seemed very unlikely, given the very strict security in force at all the national monuments in the city. But then, this was never something that would be found in any shop, and if, by some extraordinary chance, it had been for sale, Jane would surely never have had currency enough to buy it. Even to Alex's inexperienced eyes, the icon looked worth several thousand pounds.

Why did she put it in my case? She wondered. Moments later, the answer came to her, and with it a cold horror. Jane thought I would be travelling with them. She put it in my case so I'd carry it through customs. She knew the officials would never let anything like this leave the country — if she was caught with it there'd be an enormous fuss. And she was going to let *me* risk that! If customs had found it on me, quite apart from any fines I might have had to pay, almost certainly I would have been arrested and probably deported as an undesirable foreigner. I'd certainly forfeit my visa and that would mean the end of my job with Offbeat Tours. Even if I wasn't banned from Russia, the company would take a serious view of any of their tour leaders attempting anything illegal regarding customs. I'd be dismissed, for sure. And Jane would have landed me in this mess! Why?

She held up the icon and looked at it for a long time. There was a magical quality about it. She could well understand a Russian who followed the Orthodox religion, gazing into the pure, serene face of the Virgin while he prayed. Almost, she felt herself swept up in the emotion that the icon must have inspired. 'What am I going to do with you' she found herself whispering to the silver face in front of her.

Her thoughts were interrupted by a banging on the door, followed by a rattle as the chambermaid operated her pass key. Quickly, Alex thrust the icon back into her suitcase and piled some sweaters on top of it.

The chambermaid stopped short at the sight of Alex.

'Izvinitye, Madame. I had thought this room had been vacated,' the girl said in confusion.

'It's all right. I'm just moving out.' Alex closed the case and scooped up an armful of clothes from the bed. 'I'm moving to another floor. You can service the room now,' she told the girl.

In her new room, she unpacked and put away her clothes. Then she rewrapped the icon carefully in its original paper and took it down to Reception.

'Nicco,' she said to the young man on duty, 'would you please keep this in your safe for me? I can't leave it in my room.'

'But of course, Miss Vincent.' He took it from her, raising his eyebrows slightly as he registered its weight, but making no comment.

'I may need to leave it for some weeks. I don't want to take it back to England at the end of the week. Will that be all right?' Alex asked.

'Of course. You may leave it for as long as you require. We have a large safe deposit vault for our guests' needs. It will be quite safe until you ask for it.' He took it into an inner office behind the desk and on his return said 'I will give you a receipt.'

The receipt merely stated 'Large flat package'. Alex put it safely away in her handbag. She had no idea what she was going to do with the icon but she had a feeling that, after all, she might not have heard the last of Jane Chandler.

4

Alex sat in the club class section of the Pan Am plane and savoured her excellent on board meal. It was very pleasant, after a busy and rather stressful week, to feel that at last she was off duty and a whole week of freedom lay ahead of her.

The businessmen had been pleasant and friendly, but rather demanding, being keen to take every opportunity to build business links with their Soviet counterparts. Alex found that not only was she their guide but on several occasions she had been called on as interpreter. In the evenings, when she'd hoped they might perhaps dine out in a smart restaurant or in the hotel and discuss their sales strategies in the bar afterwards, they wanted to entertain the business clients they'd met and begged her to come either to interpret, or because the clients' wives were coming too, and they wanted to have a lady with them.

Sometimes the clients themselves turned out to be women and on some occasions Alex's language skills were in demand to explain products to the Russians. By the end of the week she thought she must know as much about their businesses and the import-export complications of the two countries, as any of her group. They appreciated her, there was no doubt, and both she and they were well aware that they would have found it difficult to manage without her, but it was twenty four hours a day on duty and she was exhausted by the time Boris drove them to the airport.

The check-in clerk knew Alex from her frequent previous flights, and tactfully suggested a seat somewhat removed from her group, who were busy assessing the success of their trip. Alex was grateful to be on her own at last, with no more responsibilities for anyone for a while. She read magazines, dozed, watched the Lithuanian countryside fall away beneath her, and, four hours later was informed by the pilot that they would be touching down at Heathrow in ten minutes' time and that London was enjoying a beautiful spring evening.

Her group were all seasoned travellers and so she left them to collect their luggage and disperse at the airport. Two had invited her to join them for a drink on arrival, but she had refused, pleading that a friend was meeting her. Their knowing looks made it clear that they were not surprised someone as attractive and lively as Alex had a boyfriend or fiancé waiting for her. She didn't explain further.

Richard was there when she came into the main arrivals hall. He gave her a brief but affectionate hug. 'How was your week?' he asked.

'Exhausting. I hope they don't work their poor secretaries as hard as they've worked me.'

'On call beyond the call of duty?' He raised a quizzical eyebrow.

'I should be paid several times over. Not only have I organised their visits to wherever they wanted to go, and their entertainment, but I've acted as interpreter and even escort and chaperone on some occasions.'

'They should have brought their wives,' Richard said, picking up her case.

'Heaven forbid! I should have had to find something for them to do while their husbands were doing business deals. And you can't send anyone out to window shop in Russia.'

Richard led the way out of the building. 'My car's in the multi storey. Where would you like to eat? I know a quiet little Italian place, or there's an Indian restaurant not too far — '

'Actually, Richard,' Alex said hesitantly, 'I'm really too exhausted to go out anywhere. And I had a meal on the plane.'

'Right, then. Straight back to your flat? I could cook us a snack later, perhaps. Scrambled eggs? I think I could manage that.'

'Thanks, Richard. It's sweet of you.' She realised that he probably hadn't eaten himself yet, and suggested stopping off for a take-away. The relief in his face showed that she was right, and also that he hadn't been too enthusiastic about offering to cook for her, either.

Three quarters of an hour later they were back in Alex's flat. 'I'm going to take a shower,' she announced. 'You can pour me a drink and keep the take-away warm in the oven. I won't be long. And while we eat I have a most curious story to tell you.'

Over their meal Alex told Richard about finding the icon in her suitcase. 'What on earth do you think she was playing at?' she concluded. 'I thought at first it must have been a present, but it could hardly have been that. It was far too valuable. Almost a state treasure, I should think.'

'Are you really sure about that?' Richard asked. 'It wasn't just a very clever copy of something? I've seen some good work the street sellers are offering the tourists.'

'It certainly wasn't a copy of anything, made recently! I should know, I've seen enough icons in the museums and cathedrals I've visited. It was just those, and I'm convinced it was genuinely old, too. Goodness knows where she got it from. You don't buy things like that in the Beriozka shops.'

'But why did she put it in your suitcase, if it was as valuable as you say?' Richard asked.

'That was a completely idiotic thing to do. If my case had been opened in customs, all hell would have broken loose, for sure. The Russians are very sensitive about people taking away their treasures — the Nazis took so much during the war — I'd have been taken to Moscow and thrown in the Lubianka, I should think.'

'Now you're exaggerating,' Richard laughed. 'Where is this icon thing now, anyway? If it's so valuable, how come you left it behind?'

'It's in the guests' safe deposit at the Pribaltiyakaya,' Alex explained. 'Well wrapped up, so no one can see what it is. Nicco, at Reception, knows me well and he'll make sure it's not disturbed. It'll be safe there until we can decide what to do with it.'

'All this goes some way towards explaining Jane's behaviour on the way home,' Richard said. 'You saw how anxious she became when she realised you weren't travelling back with us. She seemed terribly unsettled the whole of the journey. I couldn't understand why, but what you've just told me makes it clear now. She was expecting you to bring the icon on to the plane for her.'

'What an incredible cheek!' Alex fumed. 'I've a good mind to ask the office for her address and tell her exactly what I think of her behaviour! I certainly think the company should be warned about her. If she makes a habit of trying to smuggle illegal goods out of foreign countries when she goes abroad, she's a liability, both to the tour leader and to the travel company.'

'If this icon is as valuable as you keep saying it is,' Richard said thoughtfully, 'won't she want it back? It's my guess she'll be in touch with you before long.'

'She has no idea where I live.'

'But it would be easy enough for her to find out. She could simply go to Head Office and invent some story of having borrowed something from you, and wanting to return it. They'd probably give her your address without a second thought.'

'Do you think she really believes I brought that icon home with me? That girl can have no idea of customs regulations or of Russian bureaucracy.'

'Doubtless you'll soon find out,' Richard said. 'Let me know if there's another instalment, won't you? I'm off to the Bosphorus tomorrow; cruise of the Black Sea with twenty five tourists all yearning to see the sites of the Crimea War, plus a couple of days lazing on the beach at Yalta.'

'Have fun,' Alex replied mechanically. She knew the tour leaders all enjoyed their jobs but it was very hard work and there was very little time for fun.

'Have fun on your trips to the supermarket and the launderette this week,' Richard retorted. 'I'd better go now, it's an early start tomorrow. See you in two weeks' time, perhaps?'

'If our paths cross again so soon.' Alex stood up to see him out of the flat. At the door, she said impulsively 'Richard, I'm glad we're friends again. It was great to be working with you in St Petersburg.'

Richard took her by the shoulders, looking down into her face. 'I'm glad, too,' he said quietly. 'There must be something magical about that city.'

Alex nodded. 'There is,' she said. 'Nearly three hundred years ago it was built almost entirely by slave labour. Then, two hundred and fifty years later, a million Russians were prepared to die rather than let Hitler destroy it completely. That was his aim, you know. All those magnificent palaces were to be razed to the ground, the city wiped out.'

Richard smiled down at her. 'I see why you love St Petersburg so much. I feel sure that in a previous life you must have been a Russian defending it during the siege.' He kissed her lightly on her lips. 'See you!' he whispered, and was gone.

Alex enjoyed two days of purely domestic life, cleaning her flat, restocking the refrigerator, having her clothes washed and cleaned. She had barely returned from one of her trips to the supermarket when there was a ring at her doorbell.

When she opened the door she was not particularly surprised to see Jane Chandler standing on the step outside.

The girl looked nervous, frightened even. 'Oh, Alex, I'm so glad I found you at home!' she began. 'I called before but you were out.'

'I thought I might be hearing from you again,' Alex said dryly. 'How did you find out where I lived?'

'I asked at the Head Office of Offbeat Tours. They were a bit sticky at first but I told them you'd given me your address but I'd lost it. There was a very nice, helpful girl in their office — '

'Jennie,' Alex said with a sigh. 'Very young, very inexperienced but very willing to please. She knows she isn't supposed to give out home addresses of staff.'

'Please don't blame her!' Jane exclaimed' 'I spun her a yarn — it was all lies but I simply had to come and see you. May I come in?'

'I suppose you'd better,' Alex said ungraciously. She stepped back and Jane walked into the flat.

'Is Richard here?' she asked.

'No. Why should he be? At the moment he's somewhere in the Black Sea, I imagine.'

'Oh. I thought perhaps — ' Jane trailed off, then added 'I'm glad he isn't here. He'd probably be angry. Do you know why I've come?'

'I can guess,' Alex said grimly. 'And I don't see why you should think I wouldn't be angry. What on earth did you think you were doing, putting that package in my suitcase?'

'I'm sorry. I suppose I should have asked you first, but I thought you might say no. I'd have put it in my own luggage normally, of course, but I thought the customs officials might want to see inside my case.'

'And mightn't they want to look inside mine?' Alex strove to remain calm, though she was seething with anger.

'But of course they wouldn't need to look in yours!' Jane's wide-eyed innocence was almost too much. Alex felt like strangling the girl. 'You're always coming and going through customs at the airport. They all know you; they wouldn't ask to look in your cases.'

Alex took a deep breath. 'Don't you realise,' she said carefully, 'that I'm the person most likely to have my baggage searched? Ordinary tourists don't usually have much more than souvenirs with them, but customs know I have the opportunity for much more than that. They'd have a right to be more suspicious of me than any of the rest of the group. I can tell you, I've had my bags searched thoroughly on several occasions.'

'Oh.' Jane looked glum. 'I didn't think. Does that mean they searched you this time when you came back?'

'As it happens, no, they didn't. But it was only by chance that they didn't, I can assure you.'

Jane's face lit up. 'So you *were* all right, after all? You scared me, talking like that. I'm sorry I might have made things awkward for you, but it's all right if nothing happened. Can I have it, then? That's what I came for, to collect it.'

'What?'

'My package. I see now it was wrong of me to let you take it through customs for me, but I honestly thought it would be safer with you. I was shocked when I realised you weren't travelling back with us, but then afterwards I knew it could only mean waiting a week or so. I went to the office at Offbeat Tours and that nice girl said you'd be back at the end of the week, so I knew it would be only a matter of waiting a while. Will you give it to me, please? I can see you're busy, so I won't stay.'

Alex started at Jane as if she couldn't believe what she was hearing. 'Did you know what was in that package?' she demanded.

'Oh, yes. Mikhail showed me. It was a kind of Russian holy picture. He said they were called icons.'

'And have you any idea of its value?'

Jane shrugged. 'Mikhail said it probably wasn't worth all that much in Russia because there were so many of them, but they'd be valuable in the west.'

'I'm no expert, but it seemed clear to me that it was worth a great deal of money, both here and in Russia,' Alex said.

'I really think it rightly belongs in a museum, or one of the big churches. Do you suppose the Russians would be pleased at the idea of one of their great treasures leaving the country?'

'But they've got hundreds of them,' Jane muttered defiantly.

'Where did Mikhail get it from? Was it stolen?' Alex asked.

'Stolen? No, of course not. It belongs to Mikhail. It's been in his family for generations,' Jane said. 'What have you done with it? You *did* bring it back with you, didn't you?' She sounded suddenly frightened.

'I certainly wasn't going to risk taking something like that out of Russia,' Alex snapped. 'If I'd been caught I might never be allowed back there again. I'm not about to risk my job and my whole future just for you.'

'So where is it, then?'

'It's safe,' Alex said. 'Locked in the security deposit safe at the hotel. They don't know what it is, but they certainly won't hand it over to anyone except me, so you can forget any idea of

Mikhail trying to get it back. What in heaven's name did he think he was doing, getting you involved in such a dangerous undertaking? If you'd been caught trying to take it out of the country, you'd have been arrested for sure.'

'I don't see what the fuss is all about,' Jane mumbled. 'It's his. He can do whatever he wants with it.'

'And he gave it to you?'

'Not gave. He wanted to sell it. Look, I suppose I'd better tell you the whole story.' She looked forlorn and a little scared after what she had been told and Alex felt some sympathy for her, though she seemed astonishingly naive and not very bright. Alex, though, was anxious to learn exactly what the situation was, so she said 'suppose I make us some tea, and you tell me what this whole thing is about?'

'Thank you, Alex,' Jane said, like a small child.

When they were seated with tea in Alex's sitting room, Jane said 'I told you, didn't I, that Mikhail was my pen friend? He wrote to me first about eight

102

months ago, because he said he wanted to improve his English. It really was quite good, his written English, anyway, and I liked having letters from him. He told me how difficult things were in Russia and how he wanted to come to the west, either to Britain or America. That's why he was working hard at learning English. I think also he thought it might be easier to get to Britain if he knew someone here, or had someone to sponsor him.'

'Travel abroad for Russians isn't quite so difficult for Russians these days, since Gorbachov and perestroika,' Alex said, 'but most of them would find it too expensive. You've seen how much roubles are worth on the currency exchange and what they buy in Russia. Their money would go nowhere in Britain.'

'That's why he needed to sell the icon. Mikhail knows things like that are in demand in the west, so he thought I could take it back with me and we'd try to sell it. He said he could live for years on the proceeds.'

'He probably could,' Alex said drily. 'Is he planning to come and live here permanently? Won't he need permits, immigration papers, visas, or something? The Russians can be very obstructive about giving their nationals permission to leave the country. It might take a long time.'

'He said all he really needed was a sponsor,' Jane said. 'My father owns a factory in Kent. He would give Mikhail a job; he knows he's very clever at making things. He's a good mechanic, too. But I don't think Mikhail thought the wages he'd earn would be enough to live comfortably here, though of course they'd be much higher than in Russia. He thought having the icon would be a kind of, well, not exactly insurance, more like a pension.'

'And was it his idea to put it in my suitcase, so that I'd take it through customs without knowing I had it?'

'Oh, no! That wasn't anything to do with Mikhail,' Jane said hastily. 'I said I'd take it back with me but I was a bit doubtful about getting it through customs if it was really as valuable as Mikhail said. I thought they might wonder how

I could have afforded it. Mikhail said they are much stricter with Russians than foreigners from the west, otherwise he'd have brought it out himself when he comes. It never occurred to me that you'd have any problems, otherwise I'd never have put it in your case.'

And that was probably the truth, Alex thought. 'Jane, you really are the most incredibly naive person for your age, that I've ever met,' she said in exasperation. 'Did you really imagine that the Russian authorities would let something like that leave their country? Something as precious as that — are you sure it really does belong to Mikhail?'

'Mikhail doesn't tell lies,' Jane said truculently. 'And I know you think I've been stupid, but it's not like that at all. How are we going to get it to England now?'

'We aren't,' Alex said. 'It's staying in the safe at the hotel until I can make a few enquiries.'

'It *is* Mikhail's! Truly, it is!' Jane insisted.

'Then let him bring it to England, if he can.'

'But I've just told you! The Russians are far more strict with their own people,' Jane said. 'Mikhail says they want to know what anyone's taking out of the country, down to the last kopek. Mikhail would have problems that a British person wouldn't.'

'Well, I'm not going to risk my livelihood and possibly my freedom for the sake of an errand for someone I don't even know,' Alex snapped. 'That's final, Jane.'

Jane looked forlorn. 'He's coming to England soon, and he'll expect it to be here for him. I can't afford to go to Russia again to bring it out.'

'He'll have to manage without it. Really, Jane, you don't seem to realise what this icon is. It's not just any old picture. It's — '

'And you're an expert on them, are you? Like you're an expert on everything in Russia,' Jane said bitterly. 'All right, I'm going now. I can see I'm not going to get anywhere with you but you must surely see you've *no right* to lock it away from us.'

Alex was relieved when Jane stood up to leave but she felt quite sure that this wouldn't be the end of the matter. If Mikhail was indeed coming to England he'd certainly take a poor view of a stranger taking possession of the icon and refusing to give it to him.

'I shall be back in St Petersburg at the end of the week,' she told Jane. 'I intend to make some enquiries and find out exactly where the icon came from, before I hand it over to anyone.' How she was going to do that, Alex had no idea, but Jane wouldn't know that. 'You can tell Mikhail that it will be no use his coming to the hotel to ask for it. He may have given it to you but I've no evidence that it belongs to him. I'm not giving it up to anyone until I've investigated further.'

Jane nodded meekly. 'You'll find it really is his,' she said. 'Only — if you're Russian you don't publicise the fact that you own something like that. It could be difficult to prove ownership; Mikhail told me that so many things disappeared in the war, or were hidden away and lost, no one knows about so many of their treasures.'

'I have my ways of finding out,' Alex said, with a confidence she didn't feel. 'I know quite a few Russians who will help me.'

'Mikhail is going to be very angry when he knows I didn't bring his icon to England for him,' Jane said. She turned away and began to walk down the street. Alex watched her go slowly towards the tube station at the end of the road.

This Mikhail, she thought angrily, was prepared to let her risk a great deal for him. He sounded as if he was callously using her to gain a comfortable life in Britain. Alex wanted to tell him exactly what she thought of him, and decided that was just what she'd do, as soon as she returned to St Petersburg. Meanwhile, though Jane didn't seem to realise it, she had been saved from what might have proved a very dangerous situation. Alex was thoughtful as she closed the door and went back into her sitting room. Like it or not, she was involved now with the future of the icon, and she would have to think carefully about what to do next.

5

Alex decided to cut short her week's break and return to St Petersburg a day earlier than necessary. Hopefully, the extra time would give her a chance to find out some more about the ownership of the icon, though how she could begin to do that, she had little idea. Perhaps Boris, or Nicco from the hotel, could help her. How, without possibly bringing unwelcome publicity on herself or them, she wasn't sure.

She called into the Head Office of Offbeat Tours the morning before her intended flight, to pick up tickets, hotel vouchers and any information the company had for her concerning the coming week's tour. This time it was a specialised group of tourists; a pensioners' club who had arranged the trip for twenty of their members; all fit and able-bodied, as the report assured her, but some needing a little help in getting in and out of the tour bus.

Jennie greeted her at the outer office desk, disarmingly ingenuous. 'Hallo, Alex! Did you make contact with that young lady from one of your tours? Very anxious to get in touch with you, she was.'

'Jennie,' Alex said severely. 'Please don't give out my address to anyone who asks for it. That's confidential information. It could have been very embarrassing.'

Jennie looked surprised and rather hurt. 'But she said it was most important! And she *had* your address — she'd just mislaid it so I wasn't giving away anything confidential. And she was such a nice girl — I wouldn't have done it if it had been just anyone, I do know about Company rules. I thought I was being helpful to both of you; that you'd want me to give her your address.'

Alex sighed. 'I suppose if you hadn't, I'd have had to ask for hers, and gone to see her. Just remember not to do it again, Jennie. If I want anyone to have my address, I'll give it to them myself.'

Jennie looked suitably chastened. 'I

have all your tour details for next week,' she said, handing Alex a folder. 'But the tickets, vouchers and currency are upstairs in the other office. Caroline in Accounts looks after them.' She didn't notice Alex's expression of dismay and chattered on eagerly 'You *are* lucky, you know, Alex, to be going to all these exotic places so often, and for free. I do wish they'd take me on as a trainee tour leader, but the boss said I wasn't suitable. I know I don't speak any foreign languages like you do, but there are plenty of places where they all speak English. I'm sure he could find me somewhere nice, in America, perhaps, or Australia.'

'It's not a holiday, Jennie, I assure you,' Alex said, more sharply than she intended. 'It's hard work and a great deal of responsibility. All very well if everything goes smoothly but what if there's a crisis? Someone taken ill, or dies, even? This pensioners' group, for example. Two of them are nearly eighty. That's a bit of a worry, for a start.'

Jennie made a face. 'I know it's hard

work, but I'm sure I could do it. After all, you went on a training course for weeks, didn't you? Why won't they at least send me on one to see what I can do?'

'How old are you, Jennie?'

'Nineteen.'

'You have to be at least twenty three before Offbeat Tours would even consider you for training. And the point of Offbeat Tours is that they advertise tours to the more unusual places in the world. You could be sent anywhere; to somewhere remote where no one speaks any English. And you'd have to cope with any emergency that happened. Are you that confident?'

'Aren't there local people, guides or agents, to help?' Jennie asked. She looked very disconcerted.

'Not always. You can't count on them. My advice, Jennie, if you're really keen to be a tour leader, is to go to evening classes and learn at least one foreign language really well. Then, when you're older — '

'Thanks, Alex. I'll think about doing that. But I still think you've got a smashing job and I've got a boring one, seeing other people go off to romantic places all the time while I'm stuck here in the office.'

Alex sighed and shook her head, moving off towards the stairs. They'd never accept someone like Jennie, eager to please but scatty and immature, liable to panic if something went wrong. But she was quite competent at sorting out muddles that occurred at the office end.

Alex walked into the Accounts office and saw, to her dismay, that Caroline was alone in the room, sitting behind her desk. It might have been easier to handle the situation if there had been others around.

'I've come for the tickets and vouchers for St Petersburg next week,' she said, speaking as casually as she could. She looked at Caroline; a very pretty girl with her dark hair swept into a neat chignon, her office suit impeccably creaseless. No wonder Richard had found her attractive.

'You're leaving early, Alex. Had enough of being by yourself?' Caroline gave her a friendly smile, unaware that her words could have sounded smugly triumphant.

'I have some private business to attend to in St Petersburg before the group arrives,' Alex replied abruptly. Caroline seemed to expect her to behave as if nothing had happened, as if losing Richard to this woman meant nothing.

Caroline went across to a filing cabinet and withdrew a sheaf of papers. When she came back she continued 'I suppose it's not much fun being off duty if you're by yourself. You must be missing Richard, he's not back from the Bosphorus until after you've gone, is he?'

How convenient for you, Alex thought, seething. Did the wretched woman have to rub in the fact that she'd lost Richard? She wondered if Caroline could possibly have had any hand in arranging assignments so that she and Richard missed each other as often as possible. The Director made the final decisions but Caroline worked closely with him; she must have some influence.

'No, I'm not missing Richard,' Alex lied. 'We're just friends, colleagues, that's all. There's no reason why I should miss him if he's not around.'

Caroline's dark eyes opened wide. 'Oh! I thought you and he were an item! In fact, I thought, after your assignment a couple of weeks ago, when you were both in St Petersburg, that we'd be hearing some splendid news. An engagement announcement, perhaps?'

Alex started at Caroline in shock. 'What?' she gasped. Then, taking control of herself with an effort, she said frostily 'that's hardly likely now, is it, given the circumstances? Richard's shown me quite clearly where his interests now lie.'

'Oh, I am sorry!' Caroline looked genuinely distressed. 'I always thought — Richard's such a smashing chap and we all thought you and he made such a lovely couple together.'

Alex struggled to keep her temper. It wouldn't do to show Caroline how much she cared that Richard had finished with her.

'I'm glad you think Richard is such a smashing chap,' she said. 'A lot of other people do, too. I only hope he finds his new girlfriend appreciates him enough.'

Caroline still looked unabashed. 'He was certainly very kind to me a few months back,' she said innocently. 'He drove me all the way to Bristol — even cut short his rest break because he stayed over the weekend — '

Alex couldn't bear to listen to any more. She snatched up the papers, turning to go.

'I really don't want to hear — '

'You were away in Majorca at the time,' Caroline swept serenely on, unaware of the expression on Alex's face. 'You didn't know about the drama. Jonathan was knocked down by a car in the city centre and taken to Bristol Royal Infirmary — '

'Jonathan?' Alex asked, in spite of herself.

'My boyfriend. Well, my fiancé, actually.' Caroline blushed and gestured with her left hand. For the first time Alex noticed the large, diamond solitaire on her finger.

'I come from Bristol. My parents still live there and Jonathan is a childhood sweetheart. We met at primary school,

117

would you believe?' She giggled shyly. 'When I heard he'd been badly hurt, I was frantic. I didn't know what to do, but Richard was in the office at the time and he simply took over, explained to the Director that it was an emergency, then bundled me into his car and drove straight to Bristol there and then. Jonathan was in a bad way and I'm afraid I went to pieces over it. Poor Richard was stuck with me because Mum and Dad couldn't comfort me. He spent practically the entire weekend with me by Jonathan's bedside, holding my hand while I held Jonathan's!' She gave a shaky laugh. 'Poor Richard! Mum and Dad gave him a bed for the night but he had nothing with him, not even a toothbrush! At least I had some old things at home that I could wear, but Dad had to lend him some pyjamas and a razor. I'll never forget how kind Richard was, that weekend. He kept me sane, talking to me about anything and everything. Mainly about you. He never stopped talking about you. I had a definite impression that you and he — well, he sounded besotted with you, so I can't imagine how he could possibly have found someone else.'

Alex froze, still clutching the papers to her chest. 'I think,' she said faintly, 'I may have made an awful mistake. In fact, I think I've made a complete fool of myself.'

'You have if you've let Richard slip through your fingers,' Caroline said briskly. 'He's devoted to you — didn't you realise it?'

'How's Jonathan now?' Alex managed to ask.

'Out of danger. Out of hospital, actually. He's at home convalescing at the moment and I go back every weekend to be with him. We're getting married at Christmas. The quiet time, so the Director says! But he was good about letting me have time off when Jon was so ill, so I can't ask for more time for a honeymoon yet. And Jonathan still needs treatment. It was an awful smash. In fact, he says if I hadn't been there for him, he doubts whether he'd have pulled through. That's all thanks to Richard. I could never have organised myself to get to Bristol on my own, I was a nervous wreck. What people in the office must have thought when he rushed me into his car and roared off, I can't imagine. It must have looked as if we were eloping!' She gave a tremulous giggle.

Yes, exactly like that, Alex thought sadly. And someone who enjoyed gossip decided that was what it was, so spread a spiteful story about them. And I believed it. And Richard was so hurt that I hadn't trusted him he felt there wasn't any point in explaining. Oh, what a fool I've been!

'Alex, are you all right? You've gone quite white!' Caroline said in concern. 'Here am I, chattering on, and I never noticed you weren't feeling well. Do sit down for a moment.'

'No, I'm all right,' Alex said with an effort. 'I just felt faint for a moment, that's all.'

'Oh, my goodness!' Caroline herself went white. 'You said Richard had someone else — you didn't think he and I — If you heard about us being in Bristol but not the circumstances — oh, Alex, how awful! You surely never believed anything like that, did you?'

'No, no. Of course not. I've just remembered something I have to do urgently,' Alex replied. 'Thanks for the tickets and everything. I hope it all goes well for Jonathan'

She hurried from the office, desperate to escape from Caroline and the horrible mistake she'd made. Outside, Alex leant against the wall, shaking.

What must Richard be thinking of her? Worse still, what must he be feeling, so far away and with no chance of seeing her for at least another week? She couldn't leave things like this a moment longer.

On the top floor of Offbeat Tours offices was the planning department, where details of all the tours were worked out and information sent to tourists and tour leaders. There would certainly be a fax machine there and that was now her best means of contacting Richard.

Alex ran up the stairs and into the busy, noisy room which ran the length of the offices below. A girl, whom Alex did not know, sat at a desk near the door. She looked up from her computer terminal to ask 'Can I help you?'

'I need to send a fax,' Alex said. 'To Richard Evans. He's on the Bosphorus tour, but I don't know exactly where he is at the moment. Is it possible to contact him?'

'Let's see. Know the tour number?' The girl paused, her hand over the keyboard.

'I don't know the number.'

'Never mind. It'll be in the brochure.' The girl flicked through a thick manual with 'Offbeat Tours Presents' emblazoned on the front.

'Tour of the Black Sea and the Crimea battlefields?' she asked, looking up. 'Ugh! Sounds morbid! No accounting for taste. It started a week ago. Would that be right?'

Alex nodded. There was only one tour in that area at this time; it had to be Richard's.

The girl tapped a few keys and peered into her computer screen. 'He'll be on the boat now,' she said. 'Sailing somewhere in the Black Sea. He isn't due to land anywhere until the day after tomorrow.'

'Isn't there any way of contacting him right now? The day after tomorrow is too late.' She'd be gone; in St Petersburg by then, and faxes from Russia were fraught with complications.

'We can send a fax to the boat; no problem. But is it really urgent? The Director isn't keen on sending unless it's essential.'

'It's essential all right,' Alex muttered.

'Just write out your message and I'll get it sent straight off.' The girl handed Alex a notepad and a pen. 'Make it as brief as you can,' she requested.

Faced with actually writing to Richard, Alex's mind went blank. What could she say? And a fax was such a public way of expressing everything she was feeling at the moment.

'Buck up. Thought you said it was urgent.'

Alex picked up the pen. She wrote Richard's name and the name of the tour ship, then, before she could hesitate and be lost for words, wrote 'Richard, I've been talking to Caroline. I know all the truth about Bristol. I'm sorry. Please forgive me.'

Everything else she wanted to say was far too personal for a fax but that could wait, so long as Richard knew she understood the truth.

'That it?' the girl held out her hand for the notepad. 'Aren't you going to sign it?' she asked.

Alex added her name and handed over the notepad. The girl read it, her eyebrows rising in surprise. 'This is urgent?' she asked distainfully.

'You've no idea how urgent. Please send it. I'll pay for it myself if the Director objects.'

The girl shrugged. 'All the same to me. It'll go out at once, but I can't tell you when he'll get it. There's a time difference of five hours, I think.'

'Just so long as he gets it,' Alex said.

She went home to pack, a chore that had become almost automatic after the number of times she'd been on tours now. It would be warm in St Petersburg; the citizens enjoying their hot but very short summer.

The next day she left for Heathrow. She was taking the afternoon flight which would arrive at St Petersburg in the early evening, local time. Boris would be there to meet her, so that she could finalise arrangements with him for the bus tours they would be make making. She felt happier than she had done for weeks, but still, at the back of her mind, she fretted over her treatment of Richard.

She checked in her suitcase, then went for a cup of tea before the flight was called. She was half way through her second cup when the voice on the public address system spoke her name.

'Will Miss Alex Vincent, passenger on BA airlines to St Petersburg, please go to the information desk. Miss Alex Vincent, please!'

Alex abandoned her tea and found her way to the information desk.

'Miss Vincent? Fax for you. Sent via the Dandanelles. Lucky it got here before you left; your flight is about to be called.' The clerk handed her a single sheet of paper.

All it said was: 'Thanks for yours. Will

see you in England next week. And don't believe all you hear in future. Love you forever. Richard.'

A surge of happiness engulfed her. That last 'love you forever' showed he'd forgiven her. The rest could wait until they were both back in England.

With a light step Alex hurried towards the boarding gate as she heard her flight called.

126

6

It was almost like coming home, Alex thought, stepping out of the dingy airport building and looking across the car park to see Boris and his bus waiting for her. I'd like to live in St Petersburg, she mused, hurrying across the tarmac towards him. Where would I live? A tiny apartment somewhere in the north of the city, perhaps. I'd be rich by Russian standards, though not rich enough to live in one of the international hotels. Maybe it would be different if I was here, living like the locals. Meanwhile, I can still dream. I have two whole days to myself before the next group of tourists arrives.

'You had a good holiday at home?' Boris greeted her. 'You came back earlier than you need, surely? Your people are not due here until Friday evening and today is only Wednesday.'

'I have things to do, Boris,' Alex

explained. There were certain things to arrange for the tour, tickets for the circus or opera to buy, a local guide to hire, but these were quickly dealt with, as she had done so many times before. The icon was at the forefront of her mind.

Alex hadn't heard from Jane again since the girl had visited her at her flat. She didn't know where Jane lived, though that would be easy enough to find out through company records. But what would be the point of contacting Jane? She had said all she wanted to say to the girl and now all that was left was to return the icon to its rightful owner.

That might prove more difficult than it sounded, Alex thought. Who was the owner of such a beautiful, priceless object?

'Boris, have you heard any news reports of valuable items stolen from any museum or church recently?' she asked as they turned on to the main road towards the city.

'People are always trying to steal things,' Boris said easily. 'Why do you ask, Alex Tovarich?'

'I was wondering,' Alex said carefully. 'Have you heard of an icon being stolen, about three weeks ago? Or one of them missing?'

'An icon!' Boris laughed scornfully. 'How would anyone miss an icon? In Russia there are thousands of icons. Who would want to steal one when the country is knee deep in them?

'I don't mean an ordinary one. I mean a very old, very valuable one, encrusted with jewels and precious metals,' Alex said.

'Ah! You mean one of our national treasures! No, no one could steal one of those. They are guarded too well.'

'Where do you think I could get one?' she asked, as casually as she could.

'A simple icon; from any curio shop or street vendor. But if you want one like the ones you have seen in our churches or at the Winter Palace — forget it. If anyone would sell to you, which I doubt, you would need more money than all your rich western tourists put together, could possibly raise.'

'I thought so,' Alex nodded.

'So, be content with something made by one of the local woodworkers. They put glittering on their work and stick cut glass in many colours on their pictures. It is very pretty, some of it. Your British friends would never know differently if you tell them it is a valuable work of art.' Boris turned to wink at her.

So the mystery of how Mikhail came by the icon, deepened. The only clue she had to go on was the elusive Mikhail himself, so he must be her starting point.

Boris delivered her to the Pribaltiyskaya and promised to call for her on Friday evening in time to return to the airport to meet the next group. Alex had till then to solve the mystery.

To her delight and relief, Nicco was on duty at the reception desk.

'Miss Vincent! You have come earlier than we expected!' His face lit up with pleasure.

'I have a few things to do before the tour arrives. I never have any time to myself once I'm on duty with them,' she explained. 'And my friend Richard isn't helping me this time. He's on a tour of the Black Sea on a cruise ship.'

'Lucky Mr Evans,' Nicco commented. 'Your room is still the same one, Miss Vincent, on the fourth floor. Here is your room card.'

'Nicco, I wonder if you can help me?' Alex glanced round; Reception wasn't busy at the moment and Nicco looked as if he would appreciate someone to talk to. In fact, he beamed at her even more at the suggestion that he might be able to help her.

'Of course. I shall be glad to render any assistance I can,' he said in English.

'I'm trying to locate someone who lives here in St Petersburg, a Russian. I think I know the area where he lives and his apartment block, but it's huge, twenty storeys high at least. How can I find him? I can hardly knock on every door and ask, can I?'

'Do you know this man's name?'

'Yes, it's Mikhail. Mikhail Levchenko. I don't know any more than that.'

'You don't know his father's name, his patronymic? It is a common name,

131

Levchenko, though it is more common in the south than here, I think.'

Alex shook her head. 'I suppose there might be a concierge at the apartment? Do you have such people here, who look after all the apartments and know everyone?'

'Wait one moment, please. I will see what I can do.' Nicco disappeared into the back office and Alex wandered over to one of the brochure stands to check on the current entertainments on offer, that she could suggest to her group when they arrived.

Some moments later Nicco returned, a slip of paper in his hand. 'I think I might have what you want,' he said. 'It was a long shot, but I was lucky. Apartment 12F, in Block G. That's the twelfth floor, and there are usually about six to eight apartments on each floor. If you are lucky, there might be a name card under the doorbell, but usually not, or else it's someone's name who left years before. Ulitza Chekov. That's a street on the far side of the city, to the east. I hope he's your right Levchenko.'

'That's wonderful!' Alex said in delight, speaking in English in her eagerness. 'How very clever of you, Nicco. However did you manage it?'

'You told me the area, and I know it quite well. I looked in the telephone directory and there was a Levchenko living where you said. There were others, but not in quite that area.'

'It might be him!' Alex saideagerly. 'Thank you so much.'

'You want his telephone number?'

Alex thought, then said 'No. I can't deal with this on the telephone. I shall have to go there and see him.'

'Shall I order a taxi for you?'

It was June, the period of white nights in St Petersburg when daylight lasted until well after midnight and then there was only a slight duskiness before the full daylight of dawn. It was difficult to keep track of time under these conditions, when midnight could seem like early evening in an English summer.

Alex glanced at her watch. The time was nearly ten o'clock.

'No, thanks. I'll leave it until tomorrow.

Thank you for all your help, Nicco.'

'A pleasure, Miss Vincent.' His eyes rested on her for a shade longer than necessary. Not many girls in Russia looked like that. Alex's pale gold hair and rose petal complexion made her look typically English. If there were lots of girls who looked like that in England, Nicco thought wistfully, he must one day see if he could arrange a job transfer.

Alex ate in the restaurant and then went for a walk along by the sea wall, trying to decide what she should say to Mikhail, when — or if — she saw him tomorrow. The place was deserted, all the young people were in the city, enjoying the late opening of bars and discos in the perpetual daylight.

The problem uppermost in her mind was whether she should return the icon to Mikhail. If, as Jane had said, it genuinely was his, he was entitled to its return, and, in truth, she would be glad not to have the responsibility of it. But if he'd stolen it? If this was Britain, Alex was sure she would have gone to the police long before this, but the police in Russia were not like their British counterparts. She was not confident she would be able to explain the whole story clearly enough and if they misunderstood, she might find herself in a very awkward situation, as well as bringing trouble on a possibly innocent Mikhail.

The following day Alex took the bus into the city and went to her favourite snack bar on the Nevsky Prospekt.

Ivan and Maria greeted her warmly. 'No boyfriend this time?' Ivan's black eyes twinkled teasingly. 'He is a fine fellow, that Richard. He will make you a good husband.'

'He's not — ' Alex began protesting, then continued 'Richard's a colleague. We work together sometimes and I like him, certainly, but it's far too soon to think of him seriously. Besides, he goes to other places most of the time; I don't suppose we'll have the chance to work together again, unless we have a very large group and that's not likely.'

'But you see him when you go home?' Maria persisted. 'He very much cares for you. I saw love in his eyes when he looked at you.'

'Oh, no, I don't really think so.' Alex dismissed the remark, wishing Maria would drop the subject. The Russian woman had noticed the blush that was tingeing Alex's cheeks, however, and was not going to be distracted.

'Believe me, I know about these things,' she said. 'We see many people in this bar, young people who come in together and I get to sense things. I say to Ivan — that couple, there, they are in love, and that couple, they will quarrel soon. And, later on, we find out it is so.'

'Maria's never wrong,' Ivan joined in. 'She tells me what she thinks and later, they come in and tell us they've married, or we see them alone, just as Maria predicted.'

An idea came to Alex. 'If you're so good a judge of human nature, Maria,' she said 'perhaps you can tell me about the young couple who were in here when I came in with Richard three weeks ago. There was an English girl and a Russian man with her. Do you remember them?

136

They were in the back room and speaking English.'

'I remember,' Maria said. 'He has been in here several times since, but not again with her. But then, she was one of your group, was she not, so she would be back in England now. I think they did not know each other for very long, but she liked him. She gazed at him all the time, as though she had not seen a man like him before, though there was nothing special about him.'

'And the man?' Alex asked. She found herself waiting anxiously for Maria's judgement.

Maria said thoughtfully 'I do not think he looked a man to be trusted. Not by her, I would say. But what can it matter? She is in England now, far away from seductive Russian men.'

'Yes, she's back in England.' But was Jane safe from Mikhail's scheming? Alex found Maria's assessment of the pair of them rather disturbing.

'You were testing her powers,' Boris broke in, with a booming laugh. 'Because you don't believe what she says about you and Richard, no?'

'Of course I believe you, Maria. Except that I don't expect that I'll see Richard very often. We could quite easily miss each other every time one of us is back in England, until Christmas.'

Maria shook her head. 'No, not he. He'll find a way of being with you. You see if I'm not right.'

It was a relief when a group of customers came into the snack bar and Ivan and Maria were kept busy serving them. Alex ate her lunch, then went outside and along the Nevsky Prospekt until she came to the bus stop where she had followed Mikhail three weeks ago.

Hardly had she arrived when a bus on the same route drew up beside her. She got on, handing the driver her five kopeks and punching her ticket in the machine at the back of the bus. She had still not decided what she was going to say to Mikhail but at the moment she planned only to check out the address of the apartment. It was still early; probably he would still be at work.

Alex alighted at the stop where Mikhail supposedly lived, and walked across to the apartment block where she'd seen him go inside. Here, she came upon an unforeseen difficulty; the door had a security system which involved using a number combination, or ringing a bell in the hope that someone might let her in. At this hour, most people would be at work and she had no idea of the combination.

She stood outside, undecided, for a few moments. Then, remembering something Boris had once told her about his own apartment block, she walked round the side and came to the back of the building. This faced on to an expanse of waste ground, with several other apartment blocks round its perimeter. The place looked bleak and desolate, with nobody in sight. Alex kept walking round the building until she came to where there were several lidded refuse bins, clearly for the use of the residents. And there, beside them, was a back entrance; a small door let into the dull grey concrete wall. She turned the handle and pulled, and the door opened, Just as Boris had said was the case in his own block. Alex blessed the Russians' odd attitude to security, which led them to put high tech locks on the main entrance, but left the rear door open for residents to carry out their rubbish, or intruders such as herself, to gain entry.

There was a flight of dark and dingy stone stairs which led to the front of the building, where a rickety lift served the first fifteen floors. Alex took it to the twelfth floor, then followed a corridor that led away to the right. There were doors on either side but she could see very little because there was no natural light. The only light came from a single, bare bulb every ten yards or so, which gave out little more than a glimmer. Alex hadn't meant to come this far, when the whole apartment block seemed to be empty, but she thought she might just walk down the passage and try to locate apartment F.

Half way down the passage she noticed that there were small, metal holders screwed to each door, rather like those on the front of filing cabinets. Most of the cards in the holders were blank, or had writing so faint that it was indecipherable. Alex counted off the doors. The sixth one had no number or letter on it, but it did have a card in the holder and the writing was reasonably recent. She peered at it, wishing she had a torch with her. The Russian handwriting was poor and rather shaky but there seemed to be two names, one above the other. The lower one might possibly have been Levchenko but the name above it certainly wasn't. While she was trying to read the Cyrillic handwriting letter by letter, the door suddenly opened from inside. Alex found herself staring into the face of an elderly man. The light from behind him cast him into shadow, but she was aware of someone slightly bent, with a worn, rugged looking face and surprisingly thick, greying hair, lying rumpled on his head.

'Were you looking for someone?' he asked, in a courteous, rather beautiful voice. Alex was too startled to reply coherently.

'Er, — no. I mean, yes. I mean, not exactly looking — ' Clearly she must have the wrong apartment. Mikhail must live elsewhere.

'You are English, I think?' the man said clearly, in that language. Alex continued to stare at him, all her knowledge of Russian deserting her.

'Are you, perhaps, Jane Chandler?' the man asked. 'Please, come inside. I am delighted to meet you at last.'

Alex found her voice. 'No, I'm not Jane Chandler,' she said. 'My name is Alex Vincent. But if you know of Jane then I think I must have come to the right place after all. I am looking for Mikhail Levchenko.'

'Please, come in and sit down, Alex Vincent. Perhaps I may offer you some refreshment? Vodka, perhaps?' He ushered her inside and Alex found herself in a tiny room, cluttered with furniture which looked home made. The man indicated a wooden settle which stood against the wall, covered with brightly coloured rugs.

On one side of the room an arched

opening led to what looked like a kitchen, and in the corner of this room there appeared to be a makeshift bed. Although the place was small and poor looking, it was very clean and very neat.

The man reached into a cupboard and took down two glasses.

'Oh, no! Not vodka, please.' Alex knew that Russians often expected to drink an entire bottle of vodka at a sitting, taken neat.

'Tea, perhaps? Or coffee? It is only instant, but not too bad.' The man put the glasses back into the cupboard and went through the alcove. There he turned, and said apologetically 'I am so sorry. I have omitted to introduce myself. I am Victor Krasinski, Mikhail's grandfather. Mikhail lives with me here, but he is not at home at the moment, as you see. Perhaps I may be able to help you?'

'I'm not really sure why I'm here,' Alex began. 'I'm a tour leader, a guide for British tourists coming to St Petersburg. I met Jane Chandler when she came on holiday some weeks ago. I believe she is a friend of your grandson?'

'Ah, you speak very good Russian. I am relieved, since my English is a little rusty. I learnt many years ago but I have little opportunity to use it,' Victor said, smiling at her. 'I shall make us some Russian tea and then we will talk. I think we may have some interesting things to say to each other.'

He disappeared through the archway, which was screened by a bead curtain. Alex heard him moving about and the clatter of cups on a tray. She looked round the room. The walls were covered in pictures, framed photographs mainly of groups of men in military uniforms, but there was one picture of a woman, a rather pretty girl with her hair covered by a white scarf, in the fashion of Russian countrywomen of years ago. There were ornaments, too, rather strange ones, which looked as if they were actually parts of weapons, for they seemed to be shaped pieces of rusting metal. As her eyes roved round the room, Alex noticed a rather large space in the centre of one wall, with photographs either side and above it. It looked as if a picture had been removed recently and there was a rectangle of paler wall showing. She thought it looked about the same size as the icon.

Victor came back into the room, bearing a tray on which was a beautiful, handmade lace cloth. On top of the cloth were two fine china cups and a sugar bowl. The cups were full of a pale amber liquid.

'I believe the English take their tea with milk,' he said, setting the tray on the table. 'Unfortunately, I do not have any to offer you. Some vodka in it, perhaps?'

'No, thank you. In Russia I always drink tea like this. I prefer it,' Alex said.

He nodded. 'You are right. A ruin of vodka to put it in such a drink.' He handed her a cup. 'Now, perhaps you will tell me why you have come. Has Jane Chandler asked you to visit? Or her parents, perhaps? I hope Mikhail has not caused trouble by his friendship with an English girl.'

'No, nothing like that. It's rather difficult to know where to begin.' Alex sipped her tea and thought for a moment. She hadn't been prepared for a confrontation so soon, and certainly not with this charming, elderly man.

'Take your time,' Victor said gently. 'I have all day. I am here alone in the apartment most of the time and so it is delightful to have some congenial company. I wish Mikhail had brought Jane to talk to me. I would have enjoyed speaking English again for a while, but of course he would not bring her here. And she was with a tour; her time would have been taken up with arranged visits to our many places of interest.'

What a great shame Jane had missed meeting this lovely old man, Alex thought. And if only all the members of that group could have met him! They would have gone home with a very different perception of Russians from what most of them had arrived with.

'I understand Jane and your grandson corresponded with each other,' she said. 'Jane came on the tour mainly to meet

Mikhail, I think. She didn't seem terribly interested in seeing the churches and palaces, though of course she did come with us most of the time.'

'A great pity,' Victor said. 'But then, I am one who thinks St Petersburg is a very special place. I was one who was prepared to die to save the city from the Germans. Hitler wanted the whole city destroyed completely, but that would have been an act of vandalism we could not allow. One in three of the whole population died defending it. But I was one of the fortunate ones.'

'You were here, in the siege, during the war?' Alex asked in amazement. She had never met anyone before who had actually been in the city at that time.

'Leningrad, it was called then. The old people still use that name, with pride,' said Victor. 'It should not be forgotten. Yes, I was here then. I was a boy of twelve when the blockade began in 1941. June the twenty second it started, with attacks from the Finns in the north and the Germans in the south. I was awakened in the early hours of the morning by shellfire. We didn't know then what we to be in store for us.'

'I've seen the memorial to those who died, in the park,' Alex said. 'And I've read about the siege. But it's very low key here. No one mentions it much.'

Victor shook his head. 'We keep our memories to ourselves, deep within us. Too many of my family and my friends lie in that mass grave. But there are signs still, if you care to look, and I don't mean the marks of mortar fire on the old buildings. Have you noticed there are no really mature trees anywhere in the city? Every single one was cut down for fuel. And every blade of grass was eaten during those endless months. Do you know what else we ate? Our luxury meal was sheep gut, boiled until it became a jelly, and flavoured with clove. To this day, the scent of clove brings back so many memories.'

'I can't begin to imagine what it must have been like,' Alex said, humbly. 'But I am so very, very grateful that this lovely city was saved. I can't bear to think of the Winter Palace or the Peter and Paul

Fortress being destroyed. Or any of the other beautiful buildings.'

'I am glad you like my city,' Victor replied. 'But old men like to ramble on about the past too much, especially if they have a beautiful and attentive audience. You have not come here to have a history lesson. You have come to tell me a tale about an English girl and a Russian icon, I think.'

'So it really is yours!' If he knew about the icon, Alex felt sure it must genuinely belong to Mikhail or his family. Involuntarily, she glanced at the empty space on the wall.

'Yes, it hung there,' Victor said, interpreting her look. 'It was something wonderful and had a value that was far in excess of money. I guarded it all through the siege; it was my family's personal treasure. We called it the Icon of the Czar.'

'The Czar?'

'My father, as a young man, was a servant of Czar Nicholas, our last Czar. He was with him before the Revolution, when Nicholas and his family were taken

149

into exile, away from the city.'

'He knew the Czar?' Alex whispered in awe.

'Oh, yes. Our family were great supporters of the Czar, though we knew there was much that was wrong with the system. I am careful what I say, these days, and I do not speak of my true feelings and opinions, but I can safely say to you, Alex, my English friend, that I sometimes regret that we no longer have a royal family, as your country does. I was very happy when I heard that they have at last found the remains of Nicholas and his family and will bury him with his ancestors in the Peter and Paul Fortress. We Russians still venerate our past Czars, even though many were wicked, like Ivan the Terrible. He was not called that for nothing. We like strong leadership, even if it is harsh. We dispose of our kindly Czars; we think of them as weak.'

'The icon,' Alex said, bringing Victor back to the purpose of her visit. 'You can't really have wanted your grandson to sell it abroad?'

'Mikhail has wanted to go to the west

for a long time. He believes the streets of London are paved with gold. Well, he may be right that life would be more comfortable in London or New York but he has work and a life here, among his friends. I would not stop him going if I really believed it was the right life for him. But he wants a rich, idle life and that cannot be achieved without money, anywhere in the world. He wishes to sell the icon in the west, where it will fetch a great deal of money, and I think his friendship with the young English girl was primarily in order to help him achieve this.'

'But the icon is yours!' Alex exclaimed.

'It belongs to the family, passed down when Nicholas gave it to my father, just before the final days. It was a gift, in gratitude for his services making the ladies as comfortable as he could. He brought them things which were not officially allowed and he risked much for them. Nicholas gave him the icon and it was passed on to me when my father died.'

'Mikhail cannot sell it, then!'

Victor shook his head sadly. 'When I am dead, it will be his. He does not care about its history. He does not believe in Czars or the power of a religious picture. When we were trapped here for nearly three years, I used to look every day at that picture and it gave me the strength to keep fighting to stay alive. It has power, that I believe. But Mikhail believes in none of these things. He wants the money that it will fetch and that, indeed, would keep him in comfort in the west. It is there now, waiting for him in Jane Chandler's safe keeping. He has plans to follow her to England as soon as he can.'

'It's not with Jane!' Alex said. 'Jane was to have taken it to England but she was frightened about passing through the Russian customs with it, so she put it in my suitcase, believing that, as a regular traveller and knowing some of the officials, it would be easier for me to smuggle it into England. I wasn't travelling back with them, though and I found it in my case later. Of course, the opposite is true about customs. I'd be far more likely to be subject to a search than any of the tourists, and anyway, I realised I couldn't possibly take anything like that out of the country. It's in the safe deposit at the Pribaltiyskaya, well wrapped up so no one can see what it is.'

'You have made me happier than I can possibly tell you, Alex Vincent,' Victor said gravely. 'But you came here to see Mikhail, not me. Was it to tell him than you have the icon?'

'I came to try to find out the truth of it,' Alex said. 'I couldn't believe that he could own something as valuable as that, yet seem so casual about it. I thought it must be one of Russia's national treasures and that he'd stolen it.'

'It is a national treasure,' Victor said. 'An icon, once owned by the last Czar of Russia is a treasure beyond price. You could say, perhaps, that he stole it from me, but he would say he only stole what will be his one day. I would think, rather, that in taking it out of this country, he is stealing it from Russia.'

'It's yours. You don't have to let him have it, ever, if you don't want to,' Alex said. 'But what am I to do with it, that's the point? I can't keep it in the hotel safe indefinitely. May I bring it back to you, or wouldn't that be advisable until after Mikhail has left for England?'

'He will be angry when he learns the girl did not take it back with her. Perhaps he will go to Britain anyway; her father is a rich man and has offered him work. Perhaps, after all, he will leave me my icon. When Mikhail goes, I shall have no family here. His father died fighting in Afghanistan and his mother died when he was young. That is her picture you see on the wall behind you, my daughter, my only child. I have looked after Mikhail most of his life. Perhaps he wants riches so that I, too, may enjoy a comfortable old age, but that I doubt. However, I am content here alone if Mikhail decides to leave. Will you bring me back my icon, Alex Vincent? If I can see it again, I shall need nothing more.'

'Of course. I'll bring it back to you this evening,' Alex promised.

'No, not this evening. Mikhail will be here and I don't wish him to know it is back in the apartment. That would be too much temptation. Can you come in the day, perhaps? I shall look forward to enjoying your company and perhaps trying out my English a little? It will be pleasant to look forward to entertaining a young lady here.'

'Shall I come tomorrow? I have a group arriving in the evening and, once they are here, I shall have very little free time. But tomorrow, in the day I am quite free.'

'Tomorrow, then.' Victor stood up and took her hand. With old-fashioned courtesy he raised it to his lips. 'Dasvidaniya, Alex Vincent. I am so pleased that you came to see me.'

Alex was a little dazed as she left the apartment block. She had never expected to meet anyone like Victor Krasinski. She felt she could add him unreservedly to her growing list of Russian friends; Boris, Ivan and Maria, even Nicco, though she rarely had the chance to talk to him apart from dealing with room allocations at the reception desk. Victor was delightful, with an old-world courtesy about him that she had never met before. He would be fascinating to talk to again; doubtless he knew the city so well he would be able to suggest some completely new and different places to take the more discerning of her tour group. She was looking forward to seeing him again.

Alex spent some time in the city centre, checking on arrangements for the coming week's tour, booking the English speaking guide for a visit to the Hermitage; checking times and tickets for the circus and the Kirov ballet at the Marinsky theatre. It was early evening before she returned to the Pribaltiyskaya.

She wanted another, long look at the icon before she took it back to its rightful owner. There could surely be no harm in having it in her room overnight, instead of leaving it in the hotel safe.

Nicco was not on duty at Reception when she asked for the package. A girl was there, someone whom Alex didn't know. She took Alex's receipt and fetched the package from the safe in the office behind the desk.

Up in her room, Alex laid it on her bed and started to unwrap it. As the wrappings fell away she was looking again at the picture, this time, knowing more about its history and origins, she was looking at it as Victor must have done.

So many great and famous people must have looked on the face of the Madonna during its history. Who made it, she wondered, who had given it to Czar Nicholas, because it looked as if it must have been old even then. The Madonna's face was serene and beautiful, a little wistful but with a touch of pride in her eyes as she held her Son in her arms. It was truly a masterpiece; the artist had managed to convey so many fleeting expressions in the beautifully etched features.

Czar Nicholas had looked often at this picture. So had his four beautiful and tragic daughters, the eldest about Alex's own age when she'd been murdered. As she gazed at it, the knowledge that this icon was a link between herself and the doomed Royal family, brought the whole history of Russia in the first years of the century, closer to her. Time and again she had seen objects that had reputedly

157

belonged to the Czars, but, somehow, this icon made her feel she almost knew the family.

A knock on the door disturbed her reverie. Hastily, she threw her jacket over the icon and went to see who was there. A porter had brought a message regarding an alteration in one of the bookings for the following week. Offbeat Tours had informed the hotel that two people had cancelled at the last minute, and one single man had taken up the vacancy. The tour Director had asked that Alex should be informed that there would be one fewer passenger at the airport.

It was a trivial, routine message but Alex found she was trembling as she closed the door again. What on earth would the porter or anyone else think, if they saw such a thing in her possession? Quickly she wrapped it up again and put it at the bottom of her suitcase, covering it over with some spare clothes.

Alex left the hotel at mid morning the following day. She had asked for some strong wrapping paper and string and had parcelled up the icon so securely that it no longer looked like a flat picture, more like a parcel of clean laundry. Perhaps I'm being silly, she thought. There's no reason for anyone to guess I'm carrying anything of value. Yet she was relieved when she finally reached Victor's apartment block without incident. This time, she knew what combination of numbers to press to open the main door, as Victor had shown her. Again, there seemed to be no one around and she reached the twelfth floor in an empty lift.

Victor was waiting for her. She laid the parcel on the table and watched as, with shaking fingers, he undid the wrappings. When at last he held it up, he said, in a voice choked with emotion 'I am so very happy to see my icon again. I thought that I never would. Thank you, Alex, for bringing it back to me.' He gazed at it for a long time, then crossed the room and hung it again on the wall, over the empty, lighter patch where it had been before.

'And now,' he said 'you must take a little vodka with me, in celebration of its return.'

Alex could hardly refuse, but begged for a very small amount.

'In England, so I am told, you drink it with orange juice,' Victor said. 'I have some, especially for you, if you prefer. Here in Russia we drink it neat, which is a very bad habit.'

Alex was grateful for his thoughtfulness, and diluted her measure of vodka until it was palatable. Orange juice was not easily available here, outside the tourist shops, and she appreciated it all the more.

Victor seemed a lonely man, sitting in his tiny apartment all day by himself, until Mikhail came home from work. He seemed happy to talk to her, sometimes in his stumbling English but mostly in Russian, telling her about his life, about how St Petersburg had been when he had been growing up and it had been called Leningrad.

'We never talked of food during the siege,' he told her. 'Even now, I do not often think of it. I told you of our clove jelly, did I not, which had some nourishment, perhaps. It was a strange time, those nine hundred days when we felt as if we were alone in the world. One cannot be truly lonely again after having lived like that.'

'Look, I show you something I value almost as much as my icon.' He went across to a chest of drawers and took out a small box. He put it into her hands. 'Open it,' he commanded.

Alex was looking at something she had only ever read about. Nestling in its case was a medal, the green ribboned Leningrad medal.

'For those who were here in that time,' Victor said. 'There are not all that many of us left now, and fewer still living in the city. I am glad Mikhail did not try to sell this, though I imagine it would not fetch nearly as much as the icon.'

'Don't you think it might be better to put the icon away somewhere safer?' Alex asked. 'It seems rather a temptation to leave it hanging on the wall again.'

'You are right,' Victor sighed. 'But I like to see it there. I don't think Mikhail will take it away again. There is no one now to take it to England for him, for

I do not think Jane Chandler will come to Russia again.'

It was late afternoon when Alex finally said goodbye to Victor. She wanted to visit him again but knew that once her tour group arrived it was unlikely she would have the opportunity. She walked slowly back to the bus stop, savouring the warm summer weather, so short a season in this northern latitude.

At the hotel, she went up to her room to change, then had some tea and a brief snack. By then it was time to meet Boris and his coach and drive to the airport to meet her new group. Her two days of freedom were over.

She saw Boris's coach as soon as she came out of the hotel entrance, and ran down the steps towards him. There were the usual cluster of young men selling carved goods and painted matrioshka dolls from suitcases, standing by a wall near the road. Mostly they ignored her, knowing who she was, but she knew they were waiting for the group she would be bringing back to the hotel.

'Don't pester my tourists, please, boys,'

she said lightly as she passed them. 'They may well buy, because you've got some nice things, but they won't want to be pressured.' She smiled, including them all, as she climbed on board and settled herself next to Boris. They were a good bunch of lads, knowing when to hold back if there clearly wasn't interest, but eager for any sales and desperate for hard currency, particularly dollars or marks.

The group arrived, no more than twenty minutes late at the airport. They were a pleasant seeming bunch, elderly but mentally very alert and interested in everything. Alex greeted them, introduced herself and Boris and on the journey back to the Pribaltiyskaya outlined what they would be doing and seeing during the coming week. She missed Richard badly; the businessmen had been different and she had done her job for them, but these people were purely tourists, similar in many ways to the group that had contained Jane Chandler and the comparison reminded her of that week. Only the thought that she would be flying back with them to Heathrow at the end of the week and by then Richard would be back from the Black Sea, cheered her. This time there would be no more misunderstandings with Richard.

Of course, there was no one like Jane on this tour. They were all pensioners; a few married couples but several pairs of ladies travelling together and three lone men, who instantly chummed up and spent the rest of the holiday together.

They were a surprisingly intellectual group, opting for the opera and the ballet rather than the circus; and were thrilled to discover a performance of Chekov's Cherry Tree was on offer at the Gorki Drama theatre on the last night of their visit. The fact that it would be performed in Russian didn't seem to deter them; the play was apparently familiar enough to most of them for them to be able to follow it, even in a foreign language. Alex joined them for the performance and was in some demand as translator, but found she enjoyed the evening as much as any of them.

They arrived back at the hotel in the late evening. Most of them made for the bar for a farewell drink together, but as Alex went towards the lifts, Nicco called to her from the reception desk.

'You have a visitor, Miss Vincent. A man has been asking for you. He has been here some time, he arrived soon after you left for the theatre. He is sitting over there, in the corner.' He indicated the far side of the lounge, obscured from view by a pillar.

Alex's heart leapt. Could it possibly be that Richard how somehow managed to fly here, straight from the Black Sea, just to travel back to England with her? It was a crazy notion, but the kind of thing he might do if he had the chance of a flight here instead of to Heathrow. She hurried across the room eagerly. She couldn't imagine who else it might possibly be.

It wasn't Richard. The man who rose slowly at her approach was elderly and looked out of place in his shabby coat. Russians hardly ever frequented western hotels and Victor looked ill at ease in this one.

'Victor! How very nice to see you!' Alex clasped both his hands in hers, doing her best to show him that he was welcome. 'I'm so sorry I never managed to see you again but it has been non-stop ever since the group arrived. We fly back tomorrow morning, I'm afraid.'

Though he smiled back at her, Victor looked anxious.

'Alex, my dear, I apologise for this intrusion. I know I should not have come when you have English visitors here to look after — '

'Nonsense! I'm very pleased that you've come! I shall insist on introducing you to some of them and you can try out your English on them. But first, let me get you a drink. Will you take vodka, or would you prefer something from the west? A whiskey, perhaps?'

Victor shook his head. 'No, nothing for me, thank you. I must leave in a minute. I should not have come, but you were so kind — I had to come and tell you — '

'Tell me what? Victor, what's wrong?' At last Alex realised that the forlorn, lost look on Victor's face was not merely because he was in an unfamiliar environment.

'Mikhail has gone,' he said heavily. 'He packed all his possessions and left two days ago. I do not know where he has gone, but he has taken my icon with him.'

7

Alex was stunned by Victor's news, though on reflection, she could not be surprised. If he had left the icon in its old place on the wall, surrounded by the photos of his wartime friends, Mikhail would have seen it as soon as he entered the room. And she could not imagine Victor would be the kind of person who would hide his treasure away.

She gave what comfort she could, but there was so little she could offer. Mikhail, it seemed, had left without leaving so much as a farewell note. Victor did not think he had gone directly to England; such a journey required time to acquire visas and money, but he had given a week's notice at the furniture factory where he worked, so he must have been planning his departure as soon as he knew the icon had been returned.

Never had Alex been so unwilling to leave St Petersburg next day. If only she could have stayed on a few more days and spent them with Victor, perhaps she might have been able to learn more about Mikhail's likely whereabouts and think up some plan to help him recover the icon. Her instructions from Offbeat Tours, however, were to accompany her group back to London on the next morning's flight and see them safely on to the coach that would be waiting for them at Heathrow.

'I am sorry to have to say this,' Victor said sadly as he took his leave of her by the main doors of the hotel, 'but I fear Mikhail has used the young lady for his own selfish purposes. Worse than that, I suspect he has played on her affections and led her to believe that he is interested in her for herself, whereas the truth is that he only wishes to use her to help him get to Britain.'

'Is it that easy, to go to live in Britain?' Alex had asked.

'I do not know. But I do know that Mikhail has had this wish for a long time and made many enquiries about permits to work in the west. He seemed to believe he needed only a sponsor who would offer him a job, and some money. Now he has both, for I understand Jane Chandler's father is a wealthy man who would be prepared to find Mikhail work. And he can sell the icon for a good sum, even if he is paid only the value of the gold and jewels. All he had to do was wait until I went out to collect my pension, which I do regularly every week, and he was free to pack his belongings and the icon without interruption.'

'If he's gone to England — ' Alex began.

'He could have gone anywhere. He might have gone to Moscow first, or perhaps to the south. If he travelled into Poland, perhaps, it might be easier to enter Britain from there. I do not know.' Victor sighed. 'You have been very kind, Alex, but there is no more you or anyone can do.' He took her hand and put it to his lips in a strangely touching gesture, then walked away down the hotel steps and out into the city's twilight.

Now she was on the plane, approaching the English coastline. Alex looked out of the window and saw grey seas and a line of beach ahead. In less than half an hour they would be touching down at Heathrow, and, shortly after that, her group would be safely handed over to a coach driver and she would be free for a whole week. Richard would be back from his cruise of the Black Sea by now, and there would be time to spend together, hopefully to make up for all them misunderstandings of the past weeks. Alex forced her mind to concentrate on Richard and put all thoughts of Victor, Mikhail and the icon out of her mind. She had only partly succeeded when the plane touched down at Heathrow and she became busy helping her charges with their luggage off the plane.

She was totally occupied in finding trolleys and collecting suitcases from the baggage carousel in the arrivals hall. Some of her group were unfamiliar with the system and needed help before they were all safely aboard their homebound coach, with their suitcases stowed in the lockers beneath the seats. It was only then that Alex remembered she'd left her own suitcase abandoned in the hall while she'd helped everyone else. She went back into the arrivals hall but her case was no longer by the pillar where she'd left it.

'Bother! The airport police must have removed it for security reasons,' she thought crossly. 'Now I'll have to find their office to get it back.'

'This what you're looking for?'

She turned round, startled, to see her case held up at eye level in front of her face.

'Richard! What on earth are you doing with my case? I thought Security had taken it,' she exclaimed.

He lowered it to the ground and came forward to kiss her. 'That's not a very welcoming remark to someone who's come to drive you home — and who's hoping for a fresh beginning.'

'Oh, Richard!' Alex hugged him. 'I am so glad to see you! Am I really forgiven for being so horrible to you over Caroline?'

'If you received my fax, you know

you are.' Picking up her case again, he steered her towards the car park. 'And if you knew Caroline better, you'd know I'd never have had a hope of succeeding with her, even if I'd wanted to. She's devoted to Jonathan.'

In Richard's car, driving out of the airport, Alex relaxed against the passenger seat with a sigh of happiness. 'I'm so glad you came to meet me,' she said. 'There have been some disturbing developments regarding the icon, and you are the only person I can talk to about it.' Quickly she told Richard about her visit to Victor and Mikhail's subsequent disappearance with the icon. 'Victor is such a lovely man, Richard,' she said. 'It's a shame he can't keep his icon for the rest of his life. He ought to be able to leave it in his will to a museum instead of letting Mikhail get his hands on it. It ought not to go out of Russia.'

'It looks as if it already has,' Richard replied. 'If, as you think, Mikhail's plans are to come to England. But won't that be difficult for a Russian national? Surely it takes time and money to obtain emigration permits?'

'Victor says he has been planning to come to the west for a long time,' Alex said. 'He could have his documentation ready by the time Jane came to St Petersburg — they'd been corresponding for several months and her father had already agreed to sponsor him and offer him a job. All he needed was for her to bring out the icon for him.'

'Then the only person likely to know where Mikhail is now, will be Jane,' Richard decided. 'If he has the icon, he still has a use for her as a contact in this country. If he's here, he'll be with her or he'll be on his way to her. I feel sure of it.'

Alex shivered. 'It sounds horrible, using the poor girl like this. He can't have any real feelings for her if he was prepared to let her smuggle out the icon for him.'

'But she was going to let you take the risk for doing just that,' Richard pointed out. 'I have no sympathy for the girl. I didn't care if I never saw her again but now I think we have to. She's our only

174

link to Mikhail. Do you know where she lives?'

'No, but I can easily get her address from the records at Offbeat Tours Head office,' Alex replied.

'Then that's where we'll start, first thing tomorrow. We have a week to find Mikhail and persuade him to give up this icon. Think we can do it?'

'You'll really help to find him?'

'Try to stop me! We're in this together now. Anyway, I can see that I'll never have your full attention if I am not prepared to be as involved as you are.'

Next morning, Alex and Richard arrived at Offbeat Tours offices as soon as they opened. Jennie, at the front desk, looked up in surprise.

'Hallo! Aren't you two supposed to be off duty this week? Are you planning to spend your break taking one of our exotic holidays?'

'We've other plans, thank you,' Richard said loftily. 'We came in for some information. Can you let us have the address list of the people on the May nineteenth trip to St Petersburg, please?'

'That's easy. I'll ring through to Records and ask for a printout.' Jennie picked up the telephone. 'Be down in a moment,' she said, after a brief conversation.

'What's the next move, when we have her address?' Alex asked, while they waited.

'Go and see her, of course. Let's hope she doesn't live in the north of Scotland or somewhere equally far away.'

Moments later, a clerk arrived at Jennie's desk with a single sheet of paper in her hand. 'Here you are,' Jennie said, handing it over.

Together they scanned the list. 'What a relief!' Alex said. 'She lives near Maidstone. That's not very far.'

'Let's go now; it'll only takes us a couple of hours by car,' Richard suggested.

'What do we do when we see her?' Alex asked doubtfully. 'And do you suppose Mikhail will be there?'

'Perhaps he won't have arrived yet, though I feel sure that's where he must be heading. It will be easier, though, if we can talk to Jane alone. We might be able to persuade her to talk to Mikhail; explain that the icon rightfully belongs to Mikhail's grandfather and should stay in Russia.'

'Ought we perhaps to telephone her first?'

'No,' said Richard. 'I think we should arrive unannounced. Not give her the chance to think up excuses, or be influenced by Mikhail, if he is there.'

'If we draw a blank with Jane, perhaps we could try talking to her father,' Alex said thoughtfully, as they set off. 'I don't suppose he would like the idea of his daughter being involved with a thief, or in handling stolen property, which is what the icon is.'

They spoke little on the journey, each wrapped in thought, trying to plan what they would say to Jane when they came face to face with her. By the time they'd arrived in Maidstone, they still hadn't formed any concrete plans for approaching Jane.

In the town, Richard asked directions of a local traffic warden. 'The house is about three miles out of town,' he said, coming back to the car. 'Just off the A26. From the sound of it, it seems to be the big house in one of the smaller villages. Jane's father must be quite an important man.'

They followed the directions they had been given and some fifteen minutes later, drew up at the gates of a small but pretty, Tudor-style manor house, set a little apart from a row of cottages that made up the village.

'This must be it,' Richard said, peering out of the car window. 'It looks a rather grand place. Do you suppose they'll have a snooty butler or a parlourmaid?'

'That doesn't sound like Jane; but you can never tell. I'll open the gates and you can drive in,' Alex responded.

The drive curved round in front of the house. Richard parked a little way beyond the house and they walked back to knock on the iron studded medieval style front door.

'Are we being completely stupid, coming here like this with no clear plan of action?' Alex had a sudden attack of doubt. 'She has every right to tell us to mind our own business and refuse to discuss Mikhail or the icon, or anything.'

'And, being Jane, that's probably exactly what she will do,' Richard answered gloomily. 'But it's too late now. And we couldn't have done anything else. Victor has only us to help him.'

There were quick, light footsteps within, and the door was opened by Jane herself. She looked happier than she had done during her time in St Petersburg, and, Alex had time to notice, looked rather more attractive in consequence.

'Oh! Hallo,' Jane said uncertainly, seeing them on the step. 'I wasn't expecting to see either of you.'

'May we come in?' Alex asked.

'Were you just passing, or have you come to see me for a particular reason?' Jane sounded wary.

Alex decided it was better to be straightforward with the girl. 'We've come to see you for a reason, as you probably guess,' she said. 'Now, may we come in and talk to you, please?'

Jane stepped back and gestured for them to come inside. She showed them into a sitting room, comfortably but not lavishly furnished. Inside, the house was not as imposing as it had appeared from the outside, but was, never-the-less, a beautiful home. Clearly, both care and money had been spent freely on it.

'Would you like some tea?' Jane asked graciously. 'If you've come all the way from the other side of London to see me, I expect you could do with some refreshment.'

'Thank you. That would be very nice,' Alex replied formally.

'Please sit down,' Jane said, sounding like a polite hostess. 'I'll put the kettle on. Won't be a minute.' She disappeared into the hallway.

'So much for the snooty butler and parlourmaid,' Richard whispered after she'd gone.

'It looks like no Mikhail, either,' Alex whispered back. 'That will make things easier. If we can only get her to see that he can't keep the icon — if I could show her how much Victor cares for his

180

family's heirloom.'

A few moments later Jane returned, bearing a tray with cups, teapot and a plate of biscuits. Perhaps it was because she was acting as hostess in her own home, Alex thought, but the grumpy, truculent Jane had gone, to be replaced by a pleasant, charming though rather wary, young woman. She poured tea and handed round biscuits, then, with a touch of the old Jane, said bluntly 'Well, what was it you wanted to see me about?'

Richard took the initiative. 'It's about Mikhail,' he said. 'We heard he was coming to England and we thought you would know where he would be staying.'

* * *

Jane's face had a closed look. 'What has that to do with you?' she said rudely. 'He's come to stay in England. My father has offered him a job and paid his fare here. All his papers are in order — he's not an illegal immigrant, or anything like that.'

'Of course not! We weren't suggesting

181

he was,' Alex said quickly. 'But you see, he left St Petersburg without even saying goodbye to his grandfather and he took with him something very valuable that wasn't his. We came to ask you to persuade him to give it back to his grandfather.'

'You mean that old picture?' Jane said. 'The thing he calls an icon. Why shouldn't he bring it with him? He had to take a big risk, bringing it out of Russia himself but I let him down bungling bringing it myself, and you didn't help either, refusing to bring it or let him have it back. What else could he do? He needs it to sell, when he can find someone who will give him what it's worth. Then he'll be quite rich and — ' She hesitated, a blush creeping up her cheeks — 'We can have a good future together. Mikhail has plans for both of us.'

I doubt if his plans are for both of you together, Alex thought dryly.

'Does Mikhail know what the icon is really worth?' Richard asked.

'He says he does. He hasn't told me but it must be worth quite a lot. It has lots of gold and precious stones on it. But you know that; you've seen it for yourself. Personally, I think it's rather ugly and vulgar, but Mikhail says there are people who collect that kind of thing who would pay a lot for it.'

Jane could have no idea of what the icon truly was, where it had originally come from, or who had once owned it. But, even if she did know, would she care any more than Mikhail did, Alex wondered. She considered telling her about Victor and the icon's history. Would it frighten her into changing her mind and persuading Mikhail to return it, or would its true value dazzle her and make her all the more keen for him to sell it? Hard to tell, with Jane, how she might respond.

'That icon,' she began cautiously, and stopped. The door, left slightly ajar when Jane brought in the tea tray, opened wider and Mikhail stood in the doorway. It was the first time Alex had seen him near enough to study closely. He was a good looking young man, in a rugged, unkempt way, but his eyes, now fixed on her, were hard as flints.

'I think you are discussing me and my property,' he said coldly. 'So I think I should be present to hear what it is you are saying.'

Alex had a definite impression that he had been listening at the door ever since they had come into the room. 'That icon,' she repeated, 'belongs to your grandfather. It's a national treasure and you should never have taken it out of Russia. You certainly mustn't try to sell it.'

'How can it be both a national treasure and belong to my grandfather?' Mikhail said reasonably. 'It is true it has been in my family for some time, but it does not belong to him. My grandfather's father stole it from the Czar's home during the Revolution. Many things were taken then; after all, those people weren't going to need them any more.'

'He didn't steal it! Victor Krasinski said the Czar gave it to his father for kindnesses he did for the Czarina and her daughters, and I believe him. But anything that once belonged to Czar

Nicholas is a national treasure and ought to be kept in Russia. Do you realise its value?'

'That's why I intend to sell it.' Mikhail said with a smirk. 'But the antique shops round here have no idea even of what it is. They have offered me nothing. I intend to take it to London. You have big auction houses there and people will give me a proper price. Then I will be able to live comfortably in this country, or perhaps America, and do whatever I like.'

'Please don't try to sell it,' Alex begged. 'I went to see your grandfather — '

'And he told you some fairy tale about it!' Suddenly, Mikhail dropped into Russian and addressed Alex fiercely. 'I need the money that icon will raise! Her father promised me he would give me a job in this country. He sent the money for my fare and I think I shall be well off and perhaps I will keep the icon after all. I may not need it yet. And do you know? The man offers me work in his factory, working a machine all day for a mere pittance! I, who am a skilled craftsman in the furniture trade, and a good car mechanic. A machine minder! It is an insult!'

'I do wish you'd speak English, Mikhail,' Jane said petulantly. 'It isn't polite when I don't understand.'

'I speak Russian to make sure Alex understands,' Mikhail said smoothly. 'You see, my English is not all that good and perhaps she misunderstands what I say.'

'Then I shall say this in Russian to make sure you understand *me*,' Alex snapped back. 'Mikhail, you are taking advantage of Jane and her father and abusing their kindness and hospitality. Have you no shame?'

Mikhail shrugged. 'For years I have wanted to live in the west. I am sick of being poor and having nothing. Jane told me her father might sponsor me, help me find a job here. So what if I encourage her to think I want to come to be with her? This is a nice house and I am happy to stay here as long as it suits me. When I have sold the icon I shall buy my own house. Maybe, even, I shall not need to work; buy myself a nice car and spend all day driving round the countryside. A good, idle life. I should enjoy that.'

'You're despicable!' Alex blazed at him. She was so angry she nearly spoke in English.

'I do wish someone would tell me what you're both saying,' Jane complained.

'I was telling Alex how much I was looking forward to seeing the beautiful English countryside,' Mikhail said. 'And how happy I am to be here with you in your beautiful home. I say this in Russian because my heart is full and I cannot easily express my feelings in English.'

'You rat!' Alex said, under her breath. This time she did say it in English.

'You can see, Alex, that Mikhail plans to stay in England,' Jane said, sounding defiant. 'So he needs all the money that icon thing will fetch. If he has money it's more likely he'll be allowed to stay here. Even you must see that.'

'I see a great many things.' Alex stood up. 'I can see we're wasting our time here. We'd better go, Richard.' She was so angry she didn't trust herself to remain in the house any longer.

Richard stood up, too. To Mikhail, he said 'Frankly, I think you were brave to bring that icon out of Russia. But perhaps you aren't superstitious? You don't believe in the curse attached to it?'

'What do you mean?' For a moment, Mikhail's arrogant self confidence wavered. 'Don't be ridiculous! How could the icon be cursed?'

'Bad luck has followed all the owners so far.' Richard said. 'Look at the Czar, the first owner. He certainly had bad luck. And your father, too, I believe. Victor told Alex he died in Afghanistan — '

'I do not intend to die violently,' Mikhail said scornfully. 'This curse is rubbish. And if it is true, then all the more reason to sell it and be rid of it. Do you not think so?'

Richard shrugged. 'As I said, I admire your confidence. I wouldn't have dared risk taking it out of Russia. And Alex wouldn't, either. She was much too afraid of what might happen.'

Alex opened her mouth to tell Richard not to be so ridiculous, that she certainly hadn't any superstitious hangups, when she felt her foot being pressed under Richard's shoe. She understood his signal and bit back the retort, turning it into an emphatic nod.

'Yes, I wouldn't have risked it,' She said, with some truth. Customs officials were more likely to cause bad luck than some vague curse. She wondered what Richard had in mind.

'We won't take up any more of your time, Jane,' he said, holding out his hand to her. 'I can see there was no point in our visit. I hope your future plans work out and prove all that you wish.'

Jane shook hands mechanically. 'I'll see you both to the door,' she said, with some relief in her voice. Mikhail said nothing. He was starting after them with a thoughtful expression.

'It was at least worth a try,' Richard said gloomily as they drove out of the gate and turned towards the main road. 'Some Russians are very superstitious and I thought sow a few seeds of doubt. Frighten him a little, perhaps. It backfired, though. He'll be even keener to get rid of it now.'

'Mikhail's too tough to believe in things like curses,' Alex said. 'I did wonder, though. He did look a bit disconcerted. What are we going to do now?'

'We're going home. There's nothing else we can do. I'm sorry, love. I know you wanted to help Victor, but, short of taking the icon from Mikhail forcibly, there really isn't anything more we can do.'

'I know.' The passing countryside was a blur before Alex's eyes. It was silly to cry because they'd failed to persuade Mikhail. She might have known they wouldn't have a hope of succeeding. In spite of herself, a memory of Victor, a sad, stooped figure walking slowly down the street, the last memory she had had of him, haunted her for the rest of the journey.

Richard did his best to distract her for the rest of their off duty time. He called it making up for lost time and indeed she was happier with him than she had ever

190

been, but still, at the back of her mind, the knowledge that she had failed Victor, was always there.

At the end of the week she was off again to St Petersburg, and Richard went to Iceland. Alex travelled out with her group, members of a social club who were mostly young and seemed to have inexhaustible energy for sight-seeing. She was kept busy all the time and there was no possibility of escaping to visit Victor. Though she would have liked to see him again, she was almost relieved that she didn't have to face him and explain that there was no possibility of his ever having his icon restored to him.

After St Petersburg there were two longer trips to the south of Russia and a cruise round the Baltic to Finland, and so the summer passed. She heard no more about the icon, though she did wonder whether its sale, if Mikhail took it to one of the big auction rooms, would make the national news; the icon and its provenance were surely unique and might well be reported by the newspapers and TV. She heard nothing, however, until one day in late September, when she was in her flat preparing for her next Russian trip, the last of the season. Richard was in Moscow, on a longer spell of duty helping a series of trade delegations make contact with their business counterparts in the city. Each group came for no more than three or four days but there was so little time between them that he was staying in the city until the last of them departed at the end of the month.

Alex missed him. All their off duty time they had spent together and now it was like the first days of their friendship, happy and untroubled. He never mentioned the icon, though he must have been aware that it was often in Alex's thoughts. She suspected that he, too, hadn't forgotten but avoided the subject for fear of depressing her.

The doorbell rang as Alex was sorting through her clothes, deciding what needed to be taken to the dry cleaners before packing the following day. She wasn't expecting anyone, so it was with some annoyance she went to open the door.

She was totally unprepared for this

caller. Mikhail stood on the doorstep. He appeared dishevelled and very nervous. He looked over his shoulder several times as if he thought someone might be watching him.

'Mikhail! What on earth are you doing here? What's wrong?' Alex exclaimed.

He didn't reply, but pushed past her into the narrow passageway of the flat, shutting the door behind him. 'Is Richard here?' he demanded.

'No. He's in Moscow. He's expected back at the beginning of next week.'

'Too late,' Mikhail muttered. His eyes were darting from side to side, as if he expected something or someone to spring out from a cupboard or from behind a chair.

'Are you alone?' he asked.

'Yes,' Alex replied reluctantly. She wished she wasn't, and was about to add that a neighbour would be coming for coffee shortly, when Mikhail said abruptly 'He was right, you know. Richard said the thing was cursed. I wish I'd never had anything to do with it.'

'What do you mean? Look, you'd

better come and sit down and tell me what's wrong. Would you like some coffee, perhaps?'

'You don't have any vodka, I suppose?' Mikhail sat down but his hands were shaking. Though it was a warm day, he was wearing a heavy overcoat which he made no attempt to unbutton. In fact, he clutched it closer round himself as if he was cold.

Alex shook her head. 'No vodka, I'm afraid. Russian tea I can do, or coffee?'

'Coffee.'

He was silent while she made two mugs of coffee and brought one over to him. His hands shook but after he'd drunk half of it he seemed calmer. He looked across at Alex.

'The icon,' he said.

'I thought it might be.' Her heart was beating faster but she resisted questioning him, waiting for him to explain in his own time.

'The antique shops in Maidstone and Tonbridge were useless,' he said scornfully. 'Either they will not buy at all, or they offer me a few pounds. Useless.'

He took another drink of coffee. 'Then Jane tells me there are famous auction houses in London; Christies, Sothebys, and several others. I think, they will know the value of the icon and they will have money to buy. They will have many customers who wish to own such an object and I will make much money. So, I go to London with the icon to see these people.'

'Yes?' Alex prompted.

'What is it with you people? They ask me many questions — where I get the icon from, who owned if before me, how long I have it; so many questions. They do not talk money, only questions.'

'They need to check its authenticity. They'd ask questions about anything as valuable as that,' Alex said reasonably.

'Too many questions! I get angry. I say no more, I go elsewhere. But in all these places it is the same — questions, questions, and no talk of money! I want to sell, but they can only ask questions.'

'So you haven't sold it yet?'

Mikhail glared at her. 'You English,

you are no better than the KGB. You spy on everyone. When I go back to Jane, next day a man comes. He says he is a policeman, Special Branch. He asks me many more questions; how I come by icon, where I come from, when I left Russia, how I get icon out of Russia. Jane says she thinks he believes I steal it.'

'Well, you did,' Alex said, before she could stop herself.

'I do not steal what belongs to my family,' Mikhail said haughtily. 'But now this man says he will investigate why I am in England. He wants to see all my papers and then he tells me that perhaps I may not be able to stay in this country after all. I may come for holiday but not to live. That is no good for me.'

'So you didn't have proper immigration papers?' Alex asked.

'I have papers. They do not understand, these stupid officials.' Mikhail drained his coffee mug and held it out for a refil. Though his hand still shook slightly it now seemed to be with anger, not fear.

'So what will you do now?' Alex reached for the coffee jar and the kettle.

'I do not intend to go back to Russia. They do not like people who reject the government and try to live abroad. They would put me in the army and send me to fight. But now your government knows where I live and they want to send me back to Russia. It is all because I try to sell the icon and they think I steal it; they cannot believe I could own such an object. It is a curse on me, this icon.'

'I did wonder if it might prove difficult to sell,' Alex murmured mildly. She looked at Mikhail. 'So why have you come to me?'

'You wanted the icon — you have it,' he announced. 'They will put me in prison and then they will send me back to Russia and that will be prison again. But if I no longer have the icon they will perhaps not make so much trouble. I shall leave Jane's house and move on, before they can arrest me. I shall go to France, perhaps, or Germany.'

'What will you do for money?'

'Jane will give me money,' he said with chilling confidence. 'But you looked after the icon in Russia. Now you can do it

again. Here, take it and good riddance.'
He unbuttoned his coat and from inside
took the familiar, flat, oblong packet,
wrapped now in newspaper. He put it
down on the coffee table between them.

'No one wants it,' he said. 'And it has
proved dangerous to me. If I had not
taken it to those places to sell, no one
would have known I was here in England
without permission. But I will never go
back to Russia. Tell my grandfather that.
I know you will take it back to him
and he can have it safe for always. Tell
him — ' Mikhail hesitated, and the brash
young man image slipped, to reveal a
frightened, possibly even remorseful one.
'Tell him I wish him well, and not to
think too harshly of me.'

He stood up. 'Goodbye, Alex Vincent.
If the British police ask you about me,
you will be able to say you do not know
where I am. But you will say nothing of
the icon and they will never guess that
you have it.'

He made great play of opening the
door a crack and looking out, before
finally leaving. Alex was relieved to see

that the street was completely deserted.

After he'd gone, she went back to her sitting room and gently began to remove the newspaper wrapped round the packet. She couldn't believe it was really the icon until all the paper was off and she was gazing down at the serenely smiling face of the Russian Madonna.

'Not curse; blessed,' she whispered. 'There's something magical about you. You know your rightful place is back with Victor and I'm sure you arranged for this to happen. Now, I must do my part and see you get safely back to Russia again.'

8

Alex took the icon into her bedroom to pack in her suitcase. She didn't think there would be any real problems taking it into Russia. Her luggage, as a foreign tourist, had never been searched on entry and customs were minimal on leaving Britain. Thank goodness Mikhail came today, she thought. This was the last trip of the season; there would be no more tours of St Petersburg until next spring. In the meantime, Offbeat Tours ran holidays to warmer destinations throughout the winter. It would be difficult to find somewhere safe to keep the icon if she had to be continually absent for the next seven months.

She put the icon in the bottom of her case, then took it out again. It needed more protection from damage than merely being wrapped in paper and her clothes. Back in the sitting room she found an old, out-of-date school atlas, its covers just the right size to contain the icon, once the tattered maps had been pulled from between them. Inside the atlas, she then wrapped the icon in strong, brown paper and sticky tape.

That afternoon she went to Offbeat's offices to collect her tickets and tour information, ready for her flight the following day. Jennie handed her the folder and her tickets.

'They will be coming out independently in two days' time,' she said. 'And you'll need to meet their flight. The Boss wants you out early because there are some details to be sorted out with the local guides. It's all in the folder. Something about special arrangements for visiting the Kremlin, I think.'

'Jennie,' Alex said patiently, 'the Kremlin is in Moscow, not St Petersburg.'

'Well, I know that. But it's Moscow you're going to.'

'I always do the St Petersburg tours. It's Richard who does Moscow,' Alex explained.

'Oh, dear, have I got it wrong? Look on your ticket,' Jennie suggested.

Alex opened the folder. Inside, the airline tickets stated clearly 'London, Heathrow to Moscow, Sheremetyevo — 2.'

'That must be right; the Boss handed them to me just this morning,' Jennie said, relieved.

'Please ask him again. I can't understand why it should be Moscow,' Alex urged. She was beginning to have anxious doubts herself.

Jennie disappeared into the Director's office, then bounced back a few moments later.

'That's right,' she said. 'You're going to Moscow this time. He wants you to replace Richard who's coming back to act as second leader on an overbooked Caribbean cruise.'

'Lucky Richard,' Alex muttered. What on earth was she going to do about the icon now? St Petersburg was more than four hundred miles from Moscow.

'It had to be a man on the Caribbean cruise,' Jennie chattered on. 'Tour guides have to share a cabin on board and the other guide is Donald Wilson. He's an expert on the Caribbean. You were the only other person who can speak Russian so you have to take Richard's place.'

'But what about the last St Petersburg trip?' Alex asked. 'It's advertised in the brochure for this week.'

'It's been cancelled. There weren't many bookings and they've been offered alternative places on the spring tour, at a discount. They all jumped at it. It's likely to be snowing up there by now, anyway.' Jennie made a face. 'Sounds a really bleak place. Moscow will be much more fun, I should think.'

'St Petersburg is a wonderful city at any time of the year,' Alex told Jennie severely. 'Moscow is — well, it's interesting, but it's very much like all capital cities.'

'Never mind. You'll be back there next spring. You might even see Richard in Moscow if he hasn't already left,' Jennie said in an attempt at consoling Alex. She turned away to deal with a telephone enquiry and Alex, feeling dismissed, walked slowly out of the office.

What should she do about the icon now? She would have to take it with her to Moscow; there was nowhere safe to leave it here. Perhaps there would be some way she could manage to have it delivered to Victor. Maybe Richard would have some ideas, if he hadn't already left. She hoped desperately that he would still be in Moscow when she arrived. As well as longing to see him and ask his advice, she needed to talk to him on practical matters, since he knew the city better than she did.

The flight was uneventful, though Alex wondered uneasily if there would be problems with the icon. She was not familiar with customs procedures at this airport, unlike Pulkovo in St Petersburg. Most airports followed standard procedures for arrivals but Alex was unsure whether they were likely to be stricter in Moscow.

The plane touched down on time and taxied to the arrivals hall. Alex collected her luggage and walked towards passport control. Two officials were arguing with a swarthy looking man who seemed not to have the right documents. He had caused a bottleneck of passengers and after a few minutes' wait, a third official arrived to help. He dealt with the waiting passengers by waving through the British and American passport holders and, suddenly, Alex found herself outside the restricted zone, her luggage barely looked at.

She walked towards the airport car park, intent on finding a bus or taxi to take her into the city centre. As soon as she stepped beyond the doors, she heard her name called.

'Alex! Welcome to Moscow!'

'Richard!' She dropped her case and flung her arms round his neck. 'Oh, I'm so relieved you're still here!'

'Of course I'd be here to see you safely settled in, even if I have to fly out to the Caribbean late. Here, I've found us a taxi. We'll go straight to the hotel.'

'Richard, I've so much to tell you. But, mainly, I've brought Victor's icon with me. How I came by it again is a long story and I'll tell you later, but the thing is, how am I to deliver it back to him? There's not another tour of St Petersburg until spring and I couldn't leave it at the flat while I was away.'

'We shall have to take it to him now, before the next group arrives,' Richard said at once.

'What! It's four hundred miles to St Petersburg! And, in any case, I haven't the money for a flight ticket.'

'But the train is cheaper. In roubles it's very cheap and the exchange rate is vastly in sterling's favour. We can manage that.'

'The train? But that would take even longer,' Alex said impatiently. 'Do be practical, Richard.'

'I am being. There's an overnight train leaves every evening at ten, gets into St Petersburg about eight in the morning. We can deliver the icon and be back on the next overnight express by breakfast the day after tomorrow, in plenty of time to meet the group's flight. I can brief you on the way about what to show them, where to get tickets, and so on. Moscow is more westernised than St Petersburg. It's very easy to arrange things. And I've already hired you a tour bus with an excellent driver. You can leave most of it to him. Just read up on a few of the guide books in the meantime.'

'I've done that. What did you think I was doing most of the four hour flight?'

'Then what could be simpler? Check in at the hotel; we'll have time for a meal somewhere and I know of a place that has quite speedy service, then spend the night on the train and breakfast with Ivan and Maria if you like.'

'Do you really think it will work? Can we manage it?'

'Of course we can. Overnight we won't be spending any extra time. The Office needn't know that we haven't stayed in Moscow. Better they don't. The sooner you get rid of that wretched icon the better, I'd say. I'm beginning to believe my own inventions; perhaps the thing really is cursed. I seem to have make Mikhail think so.'

They checked into the National hotel, behind the GUM department store in Red Square. 'We're fairly near the stations here,' Richard said. 'You realise there's a different railway station depending on your destination, don't you? All part of the strange way the Russian mind works. However, they're all near together off the same square, so it isn't as complicated as it sounds.'

Alex was taking over Richard's room. His packed cases were piled neatly in a corner, the room cleaned and prepared for the new occupant.

'You weren't expecting to stay!' Alex exclaimed. 'When was your flight?'

Richard looked embarrassed. 'They wanted me home by this morning, but I insisted I couldn't leave before the group arrived. I didn't tell them I wanted to spend more time with you. I haven't seen you in ages. I told them the next available flight was in three days but that if necessary I'd forgo any leave and fly straight on to the Carribean as soon as I landed in London.'

'Thanks. I don't know what I'd have done if I'd been here by myself. I certainly would never have thought of the overnight train.'

'Sort yourself out an overnight bag. I'll see the reception desk about booking two sleepers for tonight — and a table in a restaurant.' Richard left her after a final kiss.

Alone in the room, Alex took the icon out of her suitcase and began repacking a small hold all with her overnight essentials. She wanted one last look at the icon before she parted with it for ever. She undid the wrappings and laid the jewelled picture on the bed. She was still gazing at it when Richard came back into the room.

'Everything's fixed up,' hc announced. 'We're lucky, the train isn't very full and I managed to get the whole sleeping compartment just for us. They're two doubles, upper and lower bunks, four to a compartment but there won't be anyone else using the other bunks.'

'That's a relief. I wasn't exactly relishing sharing sleeping quarters with a couple of complete strangers,' Alex replied.

'The sleepers are a bit basic, but the chap on the desk assures me they're always very clean.' He stopped abruptly, staring at the icon lying on the bed. 'Is that it? I've never had the chance to see it before.' He picked up the icon very carefully and gazed at it for a long moment. 'It really is a lovely piece of workmanship. You can see why they held these things in so much respect. It must be worth an absolute fortune.'

'So much that Mikhail wasn't able to find a buyer without honest salesmen asking awkward questions. No one would believe he could really own it and I think it frightened him that having it would land him in trouble. Your remarks about it being cursed must have had some effect, though he didn't like admitting it. And he didn't have the proper papers to stay in Britain, as we suspected all along.' Alex ran her finger along the gilded rays of the Virgin's halo. 'I shall miss it,' she said softly. 'I've always been fascinated by the story of the last Czar and his family and to think I've held in my hands something that he owned, that he looked at daily — '

They were startled by the door bursting open unexpectedly. The chambermaid stood there, her arms full of towels.

'Pardon, Madame. I did not realise this

room was still occupied — ' she began. Then her eyes went to the bed and fixed on the icon, lying gleaming in the light. She stood stock still, unable to drag them away from it. She muttered something which Alex could not catch and made a gesture with her arm, almost as if she were crossing herself.

'I'll take the towels. Miss Vincent will be using this room for the next ten days,' Richard said, reaching out for them. He moved to block her view of the icon and took the towels from her inert arms.

The spell broken, the woman bobbed an apology and scurried backwards out of the room, shutting the door with a bang behind her.

'Oh, dear, what must she have thought? She'd know I couldn't have bought anything like that in the shops!' Alex said.

'She couldn't have realised it was genuine,' Richard assured her. 'Probably she thinks everyone from the west can afford jewelled icons, and they do make beautiful ones for sale in the expensive tourist shops. Look, my case is bigger. Shall I pack it in with my gear for you?'

Alex nodded. 'Yes, please. Pack it up carefully, won't you? I don't want to give it back to Victor damaged.' She stood up, taking one of the towels from Richard. 'I think I'll take a shower before we go out to eat. I've packed the rest of my overnight things.' She went into the adjoining bathroom, leaving Richard to repack the icon.

The restaurant was pleasant, serving good Russian food and with a gypsy orchestra to entertain. They had brought their cases with them and when Richard explained to the waiter that they were catching the night sleeper to St Petersburg they were given swift and competent service, the manager promising to find them a taxi as soon as they were ready.

The train was waiting on the platform and they found their compartment without difficulty. Two two-tier bunks filled all the space, except for a narrow passageway between them. There was, however, a good sized luggage space which went back over the corridor outside.

'Enough room for all your bags if you're travelling on the Trans-Siberian route,' Richard said, indicating it. 'With our two small bags, we won't need it. But imagine spending a week travelling in a compartment like this.'

'There's quite a decent washroom at the end of the corridor,' Alex remarked, having come back from investigating it. 'And the train does seem to be nearly empty. We're travelling in luxury, by Russian standards.'

Soon after the train pulled out of the station to begin its journey, they decided to settle for the night. There was a clean pillowcase and sheeting sleeping bag provided for each bunk, and a grey, army type blanket which was so large it did duty for two.

They took the lower bunks, lying in the grey, dusky light and talking quietly.

'I gave things a great deal of thought while I was on the last assignment,' Richard said. 'It's no good, is it? We're forever bumping into each other as we pass on the way to and from foreign trips. We hardly ever get the chance to be together.'

'It's the nature of the job,' Alex said drowsily. 'We're lucky when our off duty coincides, but being together on an assignment is very unlikely. Our week together in St Petersburg won't be repeated. It's not the sort of tour that will have enough people on it, ever to need two leaders.'

'I came to a decision,' Richard continued. 'I'm going to see the Director when I get back from the Caribbean. I think he could advertise some tours that would need both of us. I have some ideas — he could incorporate them in next year's brochure — '

'Too late. They'd want me to do all the St Petersburg courses in the spring, anyway,' Alex objected.

'Then I have another plan. Why don't we start up independently, running our own tours together?'

'That would mean starting up our own company, which means having capital,' Alex said. 'This is pie in the sky talk, Richard. We'd never be able to afford to form our own company, not for years.'

'So you're perfectly happy to spend years seeing each other briefly between tours? Well, I'm not. I want to be with you more than just the odd few days. And I'm going to do something about it. Unless, of course, you are quite sure that you'd rather leave things as they are? Perhaps, for you, seeing me for a couple of days every other month is enough. If it is, tell me and I'll shut up.'

'You know it isn't.' She reached out in the gloom and felt for Richard's hand. 'I do miss you a lot and I'd like us to be able to spend more of our working lives together. But I don't see how it's possible.'

'It's possible,' Richard said. 'I've thought out a series of tours. The kind of places Offbeat like to take their clients to. I'm going to put it to the Director and suggest we team up together to lead each group. They'll be to exotic places and we'll need two tour leaders. We can make all the arrangements, just let them put the tours in their brochure and take the bookings. We'd do the rest. I'm sure they'd be interested.'

'Where would we take them?' Alex was drifting off to sleep, not paying proper attention to Richard's plans.

'The Black Sea ports; some trips to Japan and the islands off the mainland. China; the Polynesian islands, Java, Sumatra . . .'

His voice faded. Alex, who enjoyed travelling and seeing new countries, felt a frisson of excitement. Not the same city every other week, beautiful though it might be, but a whole host of new places; exotic, faraway, exciting and totally different. This was the kind of work she had dreamed of, when she had first started at Offbeat Tours.

. . . 'And we'd be together all the time. I can't imagine anything better.' Richard's voice came to her through a mist of sleep. Alex felt a warm glow of happiness. The misunderstandings, the hurt, were all behind them now. She and Richard in partnership. As soon as they had some leave together they'd work out a draft tour plan to put before Offbeat Tours Director. They'd persuade him to try it out next year; maybe even this winter if it could be arranged in time. It was sure to be a success; unusual and exotic places, such as Offbeat specialised in, but a pair of tour guides who would excel themselves to see that everyone saw as much as possible, and not only the obvious, tourist sights, but other things which would give them a flavour of how the local people lived and what they were like. It would be tours with an added dimension. It would . . .

Alex drifted off to sleep, the rhythm of the train lulling her, cocooned in her sleeping bag and blanket. Really, the bunk was very comfortable; almost as good as the hotel room she had expected to be sleeping in . . .

A sharp click jolted her into semi wakefulness. Richard must have got up to go to the toilet at the end of the corridor. But he couldn't have done, because there was still a large mound of blanket on the opposite bunk and, even as she looked, it stirred and turned over.

Alex looked towards the sliding door. Two men stood in the doorway, young, in jeans with thick sweaters. One reached towards her overnight bag, which she had left on the floor at the far end of the bunk.

'No!' She sat up, hoping that her shout would make them think again and decide to leave well alone. The man had his hand inside her bag and was feeling around.

'Where is it?' he said in Russian.

'Leave my bag alone!' Alex screamed at him, speaking in English in her indignation. To her great relief, Richard stirred and turned over. He sat up, blinking.

'What's up?' he asked.

'These two were trying to rifle through my bag,' Alex said. To the men, she said in Russian 'If you don't go, I'll scream for the guard.'

The man near the door grinned, his face reflected by the faint light in the corridor. 'The guard won't come,' he said confidently. 'We don't intend to hurt you. We only want what's in your bag.'

'There's nothing in my bag!' Alex

snapped. 'There's nothing but my overnight things and a few roubles. My travellers' cheques would be of no use to you. You'd be caught as soon as you tried to use them. If you're looking for money, take the roubles and go.'

To her horror, one of the men produced a flick knife and raised it menacingly. 'We don't want your money,' he said contemptuously. 'You know what we want. Where is it?'

'I've no idea what you mean,' Alex said in bewilderment. 'If it's drugs you're after, you've come to the wrong people. We don't deal in anything like that.'

'Acting stupid, are you?' He ran the edge of the flick knife down the side of her face, then pointed it at her throat.

'The picture — where is it?' he said harshly.

'The — picture?' Alex was so surprised she could only stare at the two men in astonishment.

'You know what we mean,' the other man said. 'The jewelled picture. You have it with you. You must have. It wasn't in your room.'

And then Alex understood. The chambermaid hadn't been as innocent as she had appeared. She must have realised at once the value of the icon, perhaps even recognised it as something too valuable to have been bought in the normal way. She had had ample opportunity to search their room for it in Alex's absence, but not finding it she would know it must still be in their possession. It would be easy enough to find out from Reception that they had been booked sleepers on the St Petersburg train, and then to send two henchmen to steal it on the journey.

Alex calculated they could not be far from Novgorod, the only stop between Moscow and St Petersburg. There, clearly, the men intended to leave, with the icon. They probably expected to take it without either her or Richard waking.

'I suppose you mean the icon?' Richard said. He was sitting on the edge of his bunk now, thrusting his feet into his shoes.

'Yes, the icon. Where is it?' One man

turned his attention to Richard while the other still had his knife against Alex's throat.

'What on earth would be the use of something like that, to you?' Richard asked them, keeping his voice casual. 'You couldn't sell it. Anyone would know you'd stolen it. It's worthless to you.'

'As it is, perhaps,' the Russian said with a shrug. 'But there is much gold and precious stones on it. Worth plenty and who could trace each jewel?'

'You couldn't!' In her anger, for a moment Alex forgot the knife touching the side of her neck. 'You couldn't possibly destroy it!'

'As your friend says, we couldn't make use of it as it is. But the stones would be enough for us. Now, hand it over or I'll cut the woman's throat.'

Richard rose slowly from his bunk. 'I suppose, in that case, I'll have to give it to you,' he said wearily.

'Richard, no!' Alex screamed. In English, she added 'He's not going to dare to stab me. Bluff him somehow. Tell him we haven't got it. Make them believe that.'

'They know already that we have it.' Richard glanced up at the luggage space over the door. 'You'll have to come inside the compartment,' he told the men. 'I can't reach to open my case while you are standing there.'

Obligingly, the second man moved past him, right inside. Richard moved so that he took the man's place in the doorway. He picked up his holdall and began to open it.

'No! Richard, don't!' Alex begged. However was she going to face Victor if these thugs got away with the icon? She couldn't bear to contemplate it.

Richard slowly withdrew the packet in its well padded wrappings. He straightened up, moved into the corridor and held it up. 'Is this what you want?' he asked.

'Yes! Da! That is it!' In his eagerness the second man lunged forward to snatch it and tripped over Richard's holdall. Richard turned towards the corridor window, which was open a little way. He pushed it wider and hurled the packet through it.

The men scrambled into the corridor, angrily shouting and swearing at him. Alex had a clear view out of the window. This part of Russia was covered with lakes and boggy swamps. Even as she watched, the icon sailed through the air and landed on the edge of a pool of water. There were a few bubbles and it tipped up to slip into the water and sink below the surface.

The two Russians ran down to the end of the corridor and disappeared through the connecting door. Moments later, the train slowed and came to a shuddering halt. There were shouts further down the line, and a door banged.

'They'll never find it, even if they can find the right place,' Richard said with satisfaction. 'This whole area is bog; it will have sunk to the bottom and so will they if they aren't very careful where they tread.'

'Richard, how could you?' Alex said, near to tears. 'We could have bargained with them — done *something*. Now it's lost for ever and it was so beautiful.'

'That icon was nothing but trouble.

We're better off without it,' Richard replied.

'How can you say that? Victor loved it. It would hardly be an exaggeration to say he worshipped it. What am I going to tell him now?'

'You'll think of something.' Richard spoke with uncharacteristic harshness. As the train started up again and began to gather speed, he added 'It looks like those two jumped off. If they go back and try to find it, they'll probably drown.'

'Richard, how could you have thrown it into the bog like that?' Alex strove to remain calm, though she was fighting back tears.

'I couldn't stomach the idea of them tearing the icon to pieces just for the precious stones and the gold,' Richard said. 'At least, this way it'll stay complete and whole. And now, if you don't mind, I'm going back to sleep.' He picked up his blanket, rolled himself up in it and lay down again in the bunk.

In moments his even breathing indicated that he was asleep. Alex lay down too but she was now far from sleepy. In the stillness of the compartment she let the tears come freely. After all the things that had happened to it, the Czar's icon had ended its days in a bog somewhere in the wild, empty wastelands between Moscow and St Petersburg. She closed her eyes and into her mind came the image of Victor, standing in the foyer of the Pribaltiyskaya, come to tell her that Mikhail had taken the icon to England. He had looked so lost and sad about it, she had vowed to herself at that moment that she would do all she could to retrieve it for him. Now she had failed utterly. No one would ever be able to find it again. Perhaps, many years hence, if there was an extreme drought, or a land drainage programme, it would be rediscovered, but by then the wooden base would have rotted away, the precious stones loosened and fallen out. It would not be recognisable for what it was, what it had been.

She tried to tell herself that Richard had acted from the best of motives. He must have believed that she would be stabbed by the knife wielding thief, though she herself felt sure it had been mainly bluff. It had all seemed so unbelievable, like a bad dream, that she had not taken seriously the danger of the knife. It simply couldn't have been happening! Now, in reaction, she felt cold and began to shiver, though the compartment was very warm.

No, she couldn't forgive Richard. He could surely have thought of some alternative ploy. He had seemed to give in so easily, producing the icon as soon as they'd demanded it.

Now she came to think about it, he had not even denied having it, not even pretended ignorance. They could both have pretended they knew no Russian and perhaps the men would have given up. Richard could have hidden his holdall under the blanket and sat on it. They might even have tackled the two, pulled the communication cord — though she had never noticed, even Russian trains must have communication cords. There were so many things they might have done to save the icon, and now, because of Richard's stupid impetuosity, they were no better off than if Mikhail had broken it up to sell in England.

The dawn came while they were still rumbling through the watery countryside, nothing but birch trees growing beside lakes and streams, and still Alex had not slept. When the scenery began to change and more buildings and factories appeared, she took her washbag and went down the corridor to freshen up before their arrival.

She shook Richard awake on her return. 'If you're going to manage a wash and shave, you'd better do it now, before there's a queue,' she said abruptly.

Richard left and she took the opportunity to put on a fresh blouse and skirt. She felt thick-headed, stuffy from the over-heated compartment and the disturbed night. She also felt deeply depressed.

In silence they picked up their overnight bags and prepared to leave the train as it drew into the station at St Petersburg. The old signboards for Leningrad were still to be seen, faded and neglected but still readable. The name conjured up visions of the wartime siege and felt in line with her mood of despair and depression.

'I suggest we go and have breakfast at Ivan and Maria's café, then go and freshen up with a shower at the Pribaltiyskaya,' Richard said. 'Might even have a swim if we can borrow cozzies from somewhere.'

Alex shook her head. 'What's the point? We might as well get the train straight back. There's no reason to have come here, now.'

'We can't get the train back straight away. I absolutely refuse to spend a whole day in a Russian train. It's bad enough spending the night in one, but at least I was asleep for most of the journey.'

'That's more than I was,' Alex snapped back at him.

'Anyway, we have to go and see Victor Krasinski. That's what we came for, remember?'

Alex rounded on him furiously. 'Have you forgotten? The icon's been lost? And all due to your stupidity! How can I go and see him and tell him that? How could I possibly face him now?'

Richard shrugged. 'Pity. I was looking forward to meeting the chap. He sounded fascinating and I wanted to hear some of his first-hand tales of living here during the siege.'

'Are you really that insensitive?' Alex stormed. 'You don't care at all, do you? You've no idea what the poor man will feel about his icon. You've no compassion.'

'I love it when you're angry,' Richard grinned. 'We shall have a great time if you yell at me when we're joint tour leaders. An extra entertainment for the clients.'

Alex glared at him. 'If you think I'd ever — ' she began.

'You sounded keen enough when we were discussing plans on the train last night,' Richard said reasonably. 'I thought that was what you wanted; what we both wanted.'

'That was before.'

'So you're blaming me because two thugs burst into the compartment and demanded the icon? What should I have

229

done? Let one of them slit your throat?'

'I'm sure he wouldn't have risked anything so dramatic. We could have bluffed our way out of it. I'd rather have died than have to face Victor. And now I'm going to have to face him. I can't *not* see him. He'd find out eventually that Mikhail had given the icon back and he'd think I kept it. I couldn't bear to have him think that.'

'We can't stand arguing on the street like this,' Richard said. 'There's a taxi. Get in.'

Alex silently opened the rear door and climbed inside. She no longer cared where it took her.

'Nevsky Prospekt,' Richard told the driver. 'Drive down it. I'll tell you where to stop.' Settling himself beside her, he said 'I'm starving, even if you aren't. We'll have breakfast at Ivan's café and then you'll feel more like planning what we do next.'

Alex remained silent during the taxi ride. She was still angry with Richard, yet she had to admit that if he *had* thought her life was in danger, he might have acted impulsively out of concern. And was there really all that much difference in the icon being at the bottom of a bog and being broken up for its jewels?

The taxi deposited them outside Ivan's snack bar. Even this early it was open, with a few customers having coffee before work.

Ivan greeted them with his usual enthusiasm. They might have been long lost relations by the way he came round the side of the counter to embrace them both.

'Maria!' he shouted towards the stairs at the back of the café; 'come and see who we have here! Alex and Richard, come to pay us an unexpected visit!'

'A flying visit, I'm afraid,' Alex said. 'I'm doing a Moscow tour, and then we don't come to St Petersburg again until next spring.'

'Ah, you miss our frozen Neva!' Ivan boomed. 'St Petersburg will be too cold for people from Britain, I dare say. Come, sit and eat! I have ham and eggs cooking. Tell me how you've been and I'll have my coffee with you while you eat.'

'We're here on a brief visit to see a friend of Alex's but we have plans for taking groups of tourists to exotic places all over the world next year, if our company's Director agrees. I think he will; I've already suggested the idea to him and he says he likes it.'

'You never told me you'd already discussed this!' Alex exclaimed.

'I couldn't let you think I'd taken too much for granted. I had to see if you were interested first.'

'You will run tours together? So you will be together all the time, not in different places?' Maria asked.

'Yes. We plan to do the kind of tours that will need two people in charge.'

'So, then perhaps you also — ' Maria hesitated, then said 'then perhaps you get married, yes?'

Alex opened her mouth to deny the suggestion, but Richard said blithely 'I certainly hope so. I sort of asked Alex to marry me on the train last night, but I haven't had her answer yet.'

'You did what?' Alex gasped.

Maria clasped her hands together in delight. 'How wonderful! No chance of a Russian wedding, I suppose? But I am delighted, all the same. But what did you say? You have come on the overnight train from Moscow?'

'Yes, that's right. This really is only a very brief visit,' Alex said.

'Then you will be in need of a shower. Why don't you come upstairs to our apartment and refresh yourselves while Ivan prepares breakfast? There is plenty of hot water and warm towels.'

'But we were going to — ' Alex began.

'That would be marvellous!' Richard said with enthusiasm. 'Thank you so much! Lead the way upstairs.'

They followed Maria up the narrow staircase to the tiny apartment above, spacious by Russian standards.

'Mind if I go first?' Richard asked when Maria showed them the tiny bathroom, a mere shower and basin at the top of the stairs.

'Come into our bedroom,' Maria

invited Alex. She was clearly very proud of the high, old-fashioned brass bedstead covered with a hand crocheted cover. There was little else in the room except a chest of drawers and a curtained off corner where clothes could be seen hanging.

'Is it really true that you marry?' Maria asked excitedly.

'I — I hardly know. Richard was talking about some scheme he had for organising unusual tours together, but I didn't think — frankly, Maria, I think I must have fallen asleep and if he did ask me to marry him, I didn't hear.'

Maria gave a great hoot of laughter, her ample hips and breasts wobbling with mirth. 'Ah! Wait till I tell Ivan! That is romantic — that is typical of the cool English!'

She calmed down after a few moments and asked in a whisper 'But do you love him, Alex? Ivan and I, we think you make a good couple, but it is not for us to make the decision. Is he the man you want?'

Alex hesitated. Could she love a man

who had hurled away into a swamp one of Russia's most valuable treasures? Could she forgive him for that, even though he might have thought the alternative was that her throat would be slit?

'I — I think — ' She'd have to forgive him first, and that would be after, long after, she'd faced Victor and confessed to him what had happened to his icon. Beside that, the past misunderstanding with Caroline seemed to pale into insignificance.

'I think I will marry him one day,' she whispered to Maria, as the water from the shower was suddenly turned off.

'Alex! Could you please fetch me a clean shirt from my holdall?' Richard shouted from the bathroom.

'I leave you now. Come down when you are ready and we will hear all your news while you eat,' Maria said. making for the stairs.

Alex reached for Richard's holdall. It was bigger than hers and seemed to contain quite a good many unnecessary items. There seemed to be no clean shirt on top, so she delved further. The only shirt she could discover seemed to be bundled up at the bottom of the bag. Really, Richard, even if this is clean it'll be terribly creased, she grumbled, pulling it out.

It seemed to be wrapped round something. She pulled the shirt away and caught her breath. Her knees felt so weak she had to sit down on the bed. Wrapped in the shirt was the Czar's icon, complete, undamaged and gleaming up at her.

She couldn't believe it. Alex sat staring at it, dumbstruck, until Richard, wearing only jeans and a towel round his bare shoulders, came to the door.

'Haven't you found my shirt yet?' He asked with studied casualness.

'I found this. What on earth — *How* on earth did it get back into your bag? I *saw* you hurl it out of the window. How could you have got it back? It *is* the Czar's icon, isn't it?'

'The very same.' Richard grinned at her expression. 'Bit of sleight of hand, you could say.' He picked up his shirt and pulled it over his head. 'I didn't like the way that chambermaid looked when she burst in and saw it on the bed in the Moscow hotel. So, when you asked me to rewrap it, I decided to wrap the book covers in the original paper and put the icon in with my clothes at the bottom of the holdall. You know, I had a funny sort of feeling that we were being watched when we got on the train, so I wasn't all that surprised when those two thugs came barging in and demanded it.'

'You planned the whole thing?'

'I didn't particularly plan to chuck the book covers out of the window, but when those two produced that knife it came to me that they'd never just accept the package, even if it looked like the icon, without checking it first. I saw the corridor window was open and I decided to throw it out on the spur of the moment. I figured we'd be here in St Petersburg before they discovered what was really in it. The package falling into the bog and sinking was a lucky bonus. If they think that was the real icon they won't go on looking for it.'

'And you didn't tell me? you let me

go on thinking you'd lost it and that I'd have to confess to Victor?' Alex didn't know whether to be still angry or not.

'I didn't want to risk telling you. Not then. There might have been other accomplices at the station. If you knew the icon was safe, your face would have given you away. You *had* to look as if the worst of all possible disasters had happened.'

'It felt like that,' Alex said. 'Oh, you can't know how relieved I am! I still can't believe this is really it, the Czar's icon safe again.'

'Not truly safe until we deliver it to Victor,' Richard reminded her. 'Am I forgiven, Alex, for putting you through so much?'

Alex nodded, putting her arms round his neck. She kissed him, and he crushed her to his chest.

'Now you're awake, and haven't other worries on your mind, I'll ask you again. Alex, will you marry me?'

Alex nodded, her head against his shoulder.

'Just as well. I think Offbeat Tours will

require a married couple to organise the kind of trips I have in mind.'

'Oh — *You*!' She hit him on the arm, just as Maria came upstairs.

'Your breakfast is waiting,' Maria said. Then she saw Alex in Richard's arms, hitting him.

'Now I know you are right for each other,' she beamed happily. 'Begin as you mean to go on, Alex, and don't let your man have the upper hand too often.'

Laughing, the three of them came down the stairs to savour the special breakfast Ivan had prepared for them.

THE END

Other titles in the
Linford Mystery Library

A LANCE FOR THE DEVIL
Robert Charles

The funeral service of Pope Paul VI was to be held in the great plaza before St. Peter's Cathedral in Rome, and was to be the scene of the most monstrous mass assassination of political leaders the world had ever known. Only Counter-Terror could prevent it.

IN THAT RICH EARTH
Alan Sewart

How long does it take for a human body to decay until only the bones remain? When Detective Sergeant Harry Chamberlane received news of a body, he raised exactly that question. But whose was the body? Who was to blame for the death and in what circumstances?

MURDER AS USUAL
Hugh Pentecost

A psychotic girl shot and killed Mac Crenshaw, who had come to the New England town with the advance party for Senator Farraday. Private detective David Cotter agreed that the girl was probably just a pawn in a complex game — but who had sent her on the assignment?

THE MARGIN
Ian Stuart

It is rumoured that Walkers Brewery has been selling arms to the South African army, and Graham Lorimer is asked to investigate. He meets the beautiful Shelley van Rynveld, who is dedicated to ending apartheid. When a Walkers employee is killed in a hit-and-run accident, his wife tells Graham that he's been seeing Shelly van Rynveld . . .

TOO LATE FOR THE FUNERAL
Roger Ormerod

Carol Turner, seventeen, and a mystery, is very close to a murder, and she has in her possession a weapon that could prove a number of things. But it is Elsa Mallin who suffers most before the truth of Carol Turner releases her.

NIGHT OF THE FAIR
Jay Baker

The gun was the last of the things for which Harry Judd had fought and now it was in the hands of his worst enemy, aimed at the boy he had tried to help. This was the night in which the past had to be faced again and finally understood.

MR CRUMBLESTONE'S EDEN

Henry Crumblestone was a quiet little man who would never knowingly have harmed another, and it was a dreadful twist of irony that caused him to kill in defence of a dream . . .

PAY-OFF IN SWITZERLAND
Bill Knox

'Hot' British currency was being smuggled to Switzerland to be laundered, hidden in a safari-style convoy heading across Europe. Jonathan Gaunt, external auditor for the Queen's and Lord Treasurer's Remembrancer, went along with the safari, posing as a tourist, to get any lead he could. But sudden death trailed the convoy every kilometer to Lake Geneva.

SALVAGE JOB
Bill Knox

A storm has left the oil tanker S.S. *Craig Michael* stranded and almost blocking the only channel to the bay at Cabo Esco. Sent to investigate, marine insurance inspector Laird discovers that the Portuguese bay is hiding a powder keg of international proportions.

BOMB SCARE — FLIGHT 147
Peter Chambers

Smog delayed Flight 147, and so prevented a bomb exploding in mid-air. Walter Keane found that during the crisis he had been robbed of his jewel bag, and Mark Preston was hired to locate it without involving the police. When a murder was committed, Preston knew the stake had grown.

STAMBOUL INTRIGUE
Robert Charles

Greece and Turkey were on the brink of war, and the conflict could spell the beginning of the end for the Western defence pact of N.A.T.O. When the rumour of a plot to speed this possibility reached Counter-espionage in Whitehall, Simon Larren and Adrian Cleyton were despatched to Turkey . . .

CRACK IN THE SIDEWALK
Basil Copper

After brilliant scientist Professor Hopcroft is knocked down and killed by a car, L.A. private investigator Mike Faraday discovers that his death was murder and that differing groups are engaged in a power struggle for The Zetland Method. As Mike tries to discover what The Zetland Method is, corpses and hair-breadth escapes come thick and fast . . .

DEATH OF A MACHINE
Charles Leader

When Mike M'Call found the mutilated corpse of a marine in an alleyway in Singapore, a thousand-strong marine battalion was hell-bent on revenge for their murdered comrade — and the next target for the tong gang of paid killers appeared to be M'Call himself . . .

ANYONE CAN MURDER
Freda Bream

Hubert Carson, the editorial Manager of the Herald Newspaper in Auckland, is found dead in his office. Carson's fellow employees knew that the unpopular chief reporter, Clive Yarwood, wanted Carson's job — but did he want it badly enough to kill for it?

CART BEFORE THE HEARSE
Roger Ormerod

Sometimes a case comes up backwards. When Ernest Connelly said 'I have killed . . . ', he did not name the victim. So Dave Mallin and George Coe find themselves attempting to discover a body to fit the crime.

SALESMAN OF DEATH
Charles Leader

For Mike M'Call, selling guns in Detroit proves a dangerous business — from the moment of his arrival in the middle of a racial plot, to the final clash of arms between two rival groups of militant extremists.

THE FOURTH SHADOW
Robert Charles
Simon Larren merely had to ensure that the visiting President of Maraquilla remained alive during a goodwill tour of the British Crown Colony of San Quito. But there were complications. Finally, there was a Communist-inspired bid for illegal independence from British rule, backed by the evil of voodoo.

SCAVENGERS AT WAR
Charles Leader
Colonel Piet Van Velsen needed an experienced officer for his mercenary commando, and Mike M'Call became a reluctant soldier. The Latin American Republic was torn apart by revolutionary guerrilla groups — but why were the ruthless Congo veterans unleashed on a province where no guerrilla threat existed?

MENACES, MENACES
Michael Underwood

Herbert Sipson, professional blackmailer, was charged with demanding money from a bingo company. Then, a demand from the Swallow Sugar Corporation also bore all the hallmarks of a Sipson scheme. But it arrived on the opening day of Herbert's Old Bailey trial — so how could he have been responsible?

MURDER WITH MALICE
Nicholas Blake

At the Wonderland holiday camp, someone calling himself The Mad Hatter is carrying out strange practical jokes that are turning increasingly malicious. Private Investigator Nigel Strangeways follows the Mad Hatter's trail and finally manages to make sense of the mayhem.

THE LONG NIGHT
Hartley Howard

Glenn Bowman is awakened by the 'phone ringing in the early hours of the morning and a woman he does not know invites him over to her apartment. When she tells him she wishes she was dead, he decides he ought to go and talk to her. It is a decision he is to bitterly regret when he finds himself involved in a case of murder . . .

THE LONELY PLACE
Basil Copper

The laconic L.A. private investigator Mike Faraday is hired to discover who is behind the death-threats to millionaire ex-silent movie star Francis Bolivar. Faraday finds a strange state of affairs at Bolivar's Gothic mansion, leading to a horrifying mass slaughter when a chauffeur goes berserk.

THE DARK MIRROR
Basil Copper
Californian private eye Mike Faraday reckons the case is routine, until a silenced gun cuts down Horvis the antique dealer and involves Mike in a trail of violence and murder.

DEADLY NIGHTCAP
Harry Carmichael
Mrs. Esther Payne was a very unpopular lady — right up to the night when she took two sleeping tablets and died. Traces of strychnine were discovered in the tube of pills, but only four people had the opportunity to obtain the poison for Esther's deadly night-cap . . .

DARK DESIGN
Freda Hurt
Caroline Lane missed her husband when he was away on his frequent business trips — until the mysterious phone-call that introduced Neil Fuller into her life. Then came doubts that led her to question her husband's real whereabouts, even his identity.